The Nomads

Jess Browning

BRONCO ePUBLISHING

Bainbridge Island, Washington

Copyright © 2012 by Jess Browning.

ISBN-13: 978-1517029586

ISBN-10: 1517029589

The Nomads

First published 2015

Keywords: ancestors, surname, nomads, history, family

Dedication and Acknowledgements

To my wife Vicki and all the members of our family who have endured the time spent by the author on the research, writing, editing, and publication of this and other books.

Table of Contents

Introduction

This story begins with a male in 1000 BC somewhere in the southwest of Eurasia. He is about 27 years old, medium height and stature with a weathered fair complexion. He, his parents, and descendants are part of a nomad tribe that have been on the move, living off the land, season following season, for as long as anyone in the tribe can remember. His wife is about 26 years old and they have two children: a boy 6 years old and a girl 4 years old. Several years ago, his wife had a stillborn child and since then has not been able to conceive.

The man has a short sword that he carries with him in a scabbard on his belt and a bow with arrows carried in a quiver slung over his shoulder. Their wagon is lightweight with four wheels and a woven hemp cover. Inside the wagon are utensils used for preparing and cooking food as well as for eating. A meager amount of clothing for the family to wear in different seasons is stored in the wagon as well as blankets for sleeping on the floor of the wagon in inclement weather or for use on the ground in better conditions. The family also carries with them their necessities including toys for the children, and various tools for leather working the horse's harnesses, preparing food, cooking, making clothes, weapons, etc. The family has several dogs and other animals that follow along.

The man has 10 horses used mostly for food and travel that are used for riding as well as for pulling the families wagon. The man is kept busy feeding and taking care of his animals and family.

The family's tribe is a warlike group composed of several hundred families. The tribe is associated with other friendly tribes that often interact in peaceful gatherings as well as in conducting war against other tribes and sometimes kingdoms.

Their wars may be in competition for land or simply for the purpose of fighting and looting. They never conquered any group in order to govern territory or people. They do however, have sacred lands that they protect and maintain for their ancestors burial and memory.

The plains of Eurasia are brown and cold in the winter, but the spring rains turn the landscape into a lush green carpet followed quickly by one of color as wild flowers come to bloom. Summer usually brings with it, nice weather.

The Concern

On a late summer evening, the family is tired after traveling with the tribe all day. For several days now, they have been moving south and westwards towards warmer weather. They are sitting around the campfire, have finished dinner and visiting with friends.

It has been a good day, the weather has been clear and warm, the sun has gone down leaving a rosy glow in the western sky, the cooking fires have died to glowing embers and the children have gone to sleep.

The husband and wife snuggle together and have thoughts of trying to conceive another child; however, they begin talking about the day and the future. His wife is concerned because the tribe's elders are talking about invading land to the west where there is great wealth among the tribes who live there. She says, "Husband, I'm worried about all the talk of invading the Cimmerian's land. They are strong willed people, and will most likely fight hard to save what is theirs. I'm afraid that many lives will be lost and many injured. It will involve all of us, and I hate to even think about those among us who may not survive or may be maimed."

The husband gave his wife's words several minutes of thought and replied, "I know how you feel about fighting, but it is our way of survival. We are Scythians, not like some of the tribes who have recently learned how to grow and harvest the food they need to survive. Our existence depends upon moving from one location to another as the weather changes. As the season gets colder, the deer and elk have to move to other locations, and as their food supply dwindles, we have to follow them. The same is true for our horses; we have to keep moving to provide them with fresh grazing land so they can continue to provide us with the necessities of life. You know that travel and fighting is our way, as it always has been. If a man, or one of his loved ones is lost in fighting, they will be remembered with honor in having lost their life in that way."

Cousin Tribes

The Cimmerians were cousins of the man's Scythian tribe and occupied land north of the Black Sea in an area located on alluvial soil between two rivers. Unfortunately, there was a great deal of hostility between the tribes. The Cimmerian tribe consisted of two groups, a royal group and common group of people. The royal group occupied the sacred land where the Scythian's ancestors were entombed and the Scythians wanted their sacred land back.

Beginning Narrative

The man's wife was concerned since the Scythians were planning to chase the Cimmerians from their sacred lands and she knew that action would only result in terrible grief. As the story unfolds several hundred years later, the Scythians invade Cimmerian land and chase the inhabitants south across the Caucasus Mountains into western Asia where both tribes become involved in conflicts sometimes opposing one another and at other times in concert against a common enemy.

Since the tribes were both mobile and warlike, they often became mercenaries, interacting with many other groups including various captives taken by the powerful Assyrians on their excursions and conquests.

The Scythians ended up ruling western Asia for 28 years although they were in the region for many more decades. The Scythians were still known and were written about for Centuries later due primarily to the fact that the region between eastern Europe and Eurasia was known as Scythia. After their sojourn in Asia, the Cimmerians preceded the Scythians into Europe becoming known primarily as Celts and the Cimmerian name, as such, disappeared from history.

The story continues as both of the tribe's ancestors migrate into Europe where they assimilated with Celtic tribes who were also their cousins. Over time they became known as Celts, Gauls, Germans, Saxons, Anglos, Iberians, Irish, Scots, and British.

Note:

The Nomadic tribes usually traveled in large wagon groups with a leader that was similar in size and organization to the much later "Wagon Trains of the West" in America. It was not unusual to see 200 wagons in a group.

They retained this type of organization into much later years as Celtic tribes who traveled looking for land, for plunder, and engaged in battles with whole families taking part.

The following Map of Scythia has been reconstructed by the author from Herodotus' "Histories".

Herodotus' Map of Scythia

Their Migration Experiences

Chapter One: Characters

Above the Black Sea in what is today the Ukraine there is a large region once known as Scythia. It is on the western edge of Eurasia bordering Eastern Europe. It was a pathway for many nomads coming out of Asia following the last Ice Age.

The retreating ice provided new opportunities as flora and fauna began to flourish in the new rich environment. The rivers and river valleys made good routes to follow due to the ease of transportation either on the water or alongside the streams. The rivers Danube, Dniester, Dnieper, Bug, and Volga were all avenues for the nomad's migrations north and west.

Over several thousand years, and in the wake of their migrations, these nomads left evidence of their passing in what has been uncovered repeatedly in archaeological digs. Many of these people buried their dead in large underground mounds constructed in a way to provide the deceased with all the comforts they might need in the afterlife. The larger the tomb, the wealthier the person had been. In these large tombs, known also as burrows or kurgans, it was common for descendants of a wealthy person, whether an elder, chieftain or king, to be buried with his horses, wife, attendants, tools, furniture, food, weapons, various implements, and other artifacts including jewelry. These burial sites have provided a good picture of what these people looked like and how they lived. Most of these people belonged to tribes consisting of a few members up to several hundred and were mostly, in some way, related. As is mostly the case, in larger gatherings, the ruling class lived separately from the more common people.

By the First Millennium BC, some of the nomads had settled between the rivers north of the Black Sea where there was abundant wildlife, wild grain, and seafood. They were learning to cultivate the soil and facilitate the growth of some of their food.

Cimmerian Narrative

Somewhat around 700 BC, one of the nomad families was associated with a common group of people and was headed by a man by the name of Ra who was about 28 years old, and like his Scythian cousin mentioned earlier, he was of medium stature and fair complexion. He and his wife Brea had four children, 3 boys and a baby girl. They belonged to the larger collective tribe known as Cimmerians.

Scythians

Many nomads passed through the region north of the Black Sea on their way north and west following the warmer climate resulting from the retreating ice. As early as 4500 BC some of these nomads began burying their dead in Kurgans near the Dnieper River. Over time one of these tribes known as the Scythians had established in this region a sacred burial ground for their ancestors.

Eventually, the Scythian's wanderlust for travel took them away from this land back to Eurasia where they had lived previously in the area between the Caspian and Ural Seas.

The Scythians were very mobile and were in the Caspian Sea region for many years while their Cimmerian cousins moved into the Scythian's ancestral lands.

A description of the Scythians comes from the writings of Herodotus, the ancient father of history, some years later (see Map page 5). His report on the Scythians says that the men were normally bearded with dark, deep-set eyes, weather-cured faces and long wind-snarled hair. They drank from the skulls of slain enemies and displayed scalps of their foes as trophies. In war and conflicts, the Scythians could be seen riding at the gallop, rapidly launching arrows from their bows. The Scythians apparently also liked to get high from marijuana. In order to cleanse their bodies, the men would make a tent by fixing sticks in the ground like an American Indian's teepee covered with woolen felts. Inside a dish was placed on the ground into which they put red-hot stones, and added hemp seed, which Herodotus said gives out vapors that no Greek bath can do better.

In another report, Herodotus wrote of Persian King Darius the Great's invasion of Scythia. Darius had crossed the isthmus between Europe and Asia near today's Istanbul and advanced on the Scythians but they kept retreating ahead of his army.

One day as both groups faced one another waiting to see what would happen, some of the Scythian tribesmen started chasing a rabbit. This infuriated Darius and he sent an emissary to the Scythian chief Idanthyrsus to ask why they refused to fight and acted in such a cavalier manner "chasing a rabbit in the face of danger".

Idanthyrsus told the emissary that his tribe owned no lands, no cities nor buildings of value worth fighting for, but if Darius ever elected to invade their sacred ancestral grounds, he would find out how well the Scythians could fight. Shortly after that, Darius withdrew his army from Scythia.

Urartu

Urartu was an Iron Age kingdom located around Lake Van in today's eastern Turkey. It rose to power in the mid-9th century BC and was conquered by Media in the early 6th century BC. It was located in the mountainous plateau between Asia Minor, the Caspian Sea, and the Caucasus mountains; an area later known as the Armenian Highlands. Its center was near the present town of Van on the banks of Lake Van. The ancient Van Kingdom was known as Urartu in Assyrian and Babylonian. In Hebrew, it was known as the biblical Ararat. It prospered from the ninth century to the seventh century BC, before being overrun by invaders.

At the end of the eighth century BC in the Near East, the Kingdom of Urartu was a strong power in the Transcaucasia region as well as the Mannae and the Medes all of which became disrupted with the advance into the region of the Cimmerians and Scythian tribes.

Arzashkun was capital of the early kingdom of Urartu, before Sarduri I (the ancient king of Urartu) moved it to Tushpa in 832 BC. Tushpa was later known as Van, which is derived from Biaina the native name of Urartu. Some ancient ruins are located just west of Van and east of Lake Van in the Van Province of Turkey, probably near the site of old Arjesh, now inundated by the waters of Lake Van. Southeast of Lake Van lays Lake Urmia which is named after the provincial capital city of Urmia, which was originally a Syriac name meaning city of water. Lake Van was known as the Upper Nairi Sea and Lake Urmia was known as the Lower Nairi Sea during the Nairi-Urartu period. Later Lake Urmia was known as the Lower Armenian Sea after the Armenians displaced the Nairi. It was also known as *Lake Matianus* and was thought to be the center of the *Mannaean Kingdom* from the ruins of *Teppe Hasanlu* on the south side of Lake Urmia. Mannae was overrun by a people who were called *Matiani* or *Matieni*, variously identified as Scythian, Saka, Sarmatian, or Cimmerian.

It is not clear whether the lake took its name from the people or the people from the lake, but the country came to be called Matiene or Matiane. Herodotus' description which has been mapped shows Matiani with Armenia to the northwest (in the same land as the Cimmerians), Assyria to the southwest, and Media to the east with the Caucasus to the north.

Assyrians

South of the Caucasus Mountains in the early first millennium BC, Assyria had become the dominant power extending from the Arabian Sea in the south to Egypt in the west, Media to the east, and Urartu to the north. Their dominion pretty well covered all of what is today known as the Near East including Turkey, Syria, Egypt, Jordan, Arabia, Iraq, and Israel.

Assyria had powerful Kings who were hungry for additional land. In expanding their empire over time, they invaded and conquered Urartu, Media, Aram-Damascus, Israel, Judah, Ammon, Moab, and the Aramean Kingdoms. If these kingdoms submitted to the will of the Assyrians and agreed to pay tribute, they were set up with a puppet government and were allowed to exist as an entity without sovereignty. If they resisted and refused to capitulate, they were conquered and their people were removed from their land and relocated to other provinces of Assyria. The former land of these captives was repopulated with people from different lands occupied by Assyria. It enabled the Assyrian to keep the land productive and better govern the captives. Although these people were initially considered captives, they were able to assimilate into Assyrian culture. Many assimilated with those whom they came in contact; and became employees of Assyrians both in public and private life. Many served in Assyria's Military. Assyria's King Sargon boasted in capturing Northern Israel's city of Samaria, that a large number of Samaria's chariots and charioteers were incorporated into his army.[1] Not only did the Assyrian kings use captive peoples in their army, they also used mercenary tribes who were used to warfare and fighting on horseback. Proof that the Assyrians used Cimmerians in their army as mercenaries is shown in a legal document of 679 BC. It refers to an Assyrian *commander of the Cimmerian regiment.* In other Assyrian documents, they refer to the Cimmerians as *the seed of runaways who know neither vows to the gods nor oaths.*

---

[1] See index in *Ancient European Ancestors: The DNA*, Archaeological, Historic, and Linguistic Evidence.

Media

The ancient country of Media was located in what later became known as Persia then in later years became known politically as Iran. It was located to the northeastern section of present-day Iran and their religion included a priestly caste called the Magi. The people of Media like the Scythians spoke a dialect of Aryan language, which was a branch of the Indo-European language. The word Iran means people from Arya.

In northern Iran and parts of Iraq, Turkey, Armenia, and Azerbijian in the region of Kurdistan some people still speak the old Scythian dialect.

Today northwest of the Iranian city of Saqqez (Seqiz) the region is inhabited by Gawirk Kurds. Iranian Kurdistan is an unofficial name for the parts of Iran inhabited by Kurds and has borders with Iraq and Turkey. According to the Kurds their ancient Iranian ancestors have lived in Saqqez and surrounding areas since approximately 1000 BC. In the pre-Islamic era, Saqqez and surrounding areas comprised a small country known as Sagapeni, which is believed to be related to the name of the ancient Sakas (Scythians) from which the name of the city is derived.

North of Media there is a plain intersected by rivers, the largest being the Cyrus, which has its beginning in Armenia. The river flows into the plain and merges with the Araxes River, which flows from the Caucasus Mountains; through a narrow valley in great volume; through fertile plains receiving more rivers; and empties into the Caspian Sea.

An archaeological dig on the south shore of the Caspian Sea, revealed a highly developed culture dating from the seventh century BC. The excavation uncovered dwellings with stone foundations and wooden walls and roofs and many graves, which yielded more than 640 objects, including gold vessels and ornaments, bronze and iron tools and weapons, and ceramic jars and figurines. The style of the gold specimens indicates that its inhabitants probably traded with the Scythians of southern Russia to the north and the Medians of the Luristan region to the south, in addition to others.

Babylonia

Babylon was a smaller kingdom in the region, although still powerful, and there was much interaction between the royal families of Assyria and Babylon. However, arguments and infighting between these royals led to Assyria's downfall.

In the year 612 BC, a coalition army made up of Babylonians, Meads, and Scythians put the Assyrian city of Nineveh under siege eventually capturing it and all the inhabitants. Babylon then took over and continued, to a lesser degree, the expansionary tactics of the Assyrians, which led to the capture, and exile of the Kingdom of Judah to Babylon in 589 BC.

Later, in 539 BC, the Persian King Cyrus conquered Babylon and allowed the Judaites to return, with their religion intact, to Jerusalem.

Levant

The Levant describes the Eastern Mediterranean at large, but can be used as a geographical term that denotes a large area in Western Asia formed by the lands bordering the eastern shores of the Mediterranean.

Historically the Levant included Phoenicia, Canaan, Syria, and the Hebrew tribes who later became known as the Israelites and Jews.

Canaan was the land that the Prophet Abram was promised and was told by God that his seed would bring forth many kingdoms and more people than the sand on ocean's shores.

Their Migration Experiences

Chapter Two: The Invasion

In the latter part of the 8th century BC, preparations were being made for war. The Scythians had decided to return to their land and push the Cimmerian tribes out of the Scythian's sacred ancestral grounds.

Leading up to the Scythian's invasion of their sacred homeland, some of the common Cimmerians traveled west and settled in the Thracian regions.

When the Cimmerians fled into Asia to escape the Scythians, part of them settled on the south shore of the Black Sea at Sinope, a city that has had the same name since the beginning of written history.

Some of the other Cimmerians settled in an area south of the Darial Gorge in a place that came to be known as Gyumri that was named for them.

Also, following the invasion, some of the Scythians settled southwest of the Derbent passage. Locations as well as rulers of the time are described below.

The Black Sea

As noted earlier, the area north of the Black Sea had been the home for many nomad tribes transiting the region. The Black Sea is the dividing line between Eastern Europe and Western Asia. In antiquity, the Black Sea has been referred to as the *Inland Sea*, the *Sea of Ashkenaz* and the *Euxino Pontus*. It was a barrier to migration south for the nomads coming out of Eurasia but, they never tried too hard to circumvent the Sea since the region to north offered rich fertile land that supported the nomad's way of life. There were several ways however in which to migrate into Asia - one to the west and two to the east of the Black Sea.

The Caspian Sea

The Scythians had been living south of the Caspian Sea in the country of the Medes for years since leaving their last homeland north of the Black Sea in territory occupied by the Cimmerians. Life had been good as the tribe moved back and forth with the seasons north and south in the region between the Caspian and Aral Seas. When not foraging for food on the broad plains, the tribe became great fishermen and lived off the food taken from the Caspian and Ural seas. They were exceptional consumers of fish and some of them were called the "Apa-saca", meaning the water Saca.

Cimmerian Bosporus

Some authors say, in the region north of the Black Sea, the Crimea is named after the Cimmerians. Herodotus, the famous father of history, reports that during his time "Scythia still retained traces of the Cimmerians": there were Cimmerian castles and a Cimmerian ferry; also a tract of land called Cimmeria and the Cimmerian Bosporus.

The Caucasus

The ancient kingdoms of the region included Armenia, Iberia (an ancient name of the Caucasus), Urartu and Albania and others. These kingdoms were later incorporated into empires, including the Assyrian, Achaemenid, Parthian, and Sassanid.

Zoroastrianism followed later by Eastern Christianity were the dominant religions in the region.

The Caucasus region from about 2100 to 750 BC survived invasions by the Hittites, Urartians, and Medes. In the Median period, beginning in the 8th century BC, it experienced successive Cimmerian and Scythian invasions.

The presence of such invaders is attested by burials

and other characteristic artifacts excavated at various 7th century BC sites in the region.

In central Georgia, archaeologists have found the greatest concentration of materials of the Scythian type from about 700 BC. This area apparently served as a base for further incursions to the south and west.

Scattered Scythian colonies may have survived there and in adjacent regions for some generations and are possibly reflected in tribal names. In addition to Saka, there was a tribe called *Skythenoi* living in the ancient Armenian region of the Coruh valley which is mentioned by Xenophon and later authors.

Today's Coruh River begins in northeastern Turkey and flows through gorges before flowing into Georgia, where it reaches the Black Sea a few kilometers north of the Turkish-Georgian border near today's Batumi in Georgia .

Cimmerian Kings

During the eight century BC, and the years following, the Cimmerian's were led by kings whose names have been interpreted and recorded by ancient authors. King Lygdamis who reigned from about 720 to 690 BC led the Cimmerians into Asia.

One of the more famous kings was Tueshpa. He was also known as king of the Gimarri and reigned from 680 to 670 BC. The name Tueshpa comes from Iranian and means "swelling with strength". He was mentioned in the annals of Assyrian King Esarhaddon.

Following him was King Tugdamme whose legacy began sometime around 660 BC. Tugdamme in Iranian means "giving happiness".

Ashurbanipal's inscriptions show that King Tugdamme was killed in battle and that his son Sandakuru survived. Both Tugdamme and his son Sandakuru had Iranian names since Sandakuru in Iranian means "Splendid Son". The word is still in use today's Kurdish language meaning son.

Sandakuru is associated with Cyaxares and his son Astyages who ruled about 610 BC which associates Tugdamme with Phraortes, the Median king.

Most historians think that Tugdamme was a Cimmerian king but the Assyrian inscriptions speak of him as being the King of the Saka. The Assyrians also called him King of Kish or King of the world which suggests that Tugdamme ruled a vast area of land.

Confusion of the tribal names may be attributed to the term Umma-Manda which has a barbarian connotation – "a numerous horde".

Tugdamme was defeated about 641 BC, but it remains unknown as to who defeated and killed him. The historian Strabo suggests that Lydia's

King Madys killed Tugdamme and defeated his forces.

Following Tueshpa came King Getmalor who reigned about 677 BC. Much later, King Antenor the First, also known as Euxim, was born about 483 BC and died about 443 BC. He reigned as king of the Cimmerians and was called "Chief Prince of Ephraim". He was said to be of Trojan Blood. He was followed by Marcomir who was born about 460 BC and died about 396 BC.

Marcomir was said to have brought his people out of Scythia across the lands of the Danube into Gaul, which they conquered and settled. One of his sons, recorded as Antenor the Second, was born about 442 BC and died about 384 BC.

Scythian Kings

Following the encounter with the Cimmerians, the Scythians were led by various kings whose names have been interpreted and described by various authors in works of ancient history.

They include Ispakaia, the Scythian king who lived from 699 to 675 BC. He led the Scythians in their second encounter with the Cimmerians and was an ally of the kingdoms of Mannae and Urartu in the Near East. In 676 BC, Esarhaddon took the towns of Sissu and Kundu in the Taurus Mountains south of the Caucasus Mountains. His oracle-text inscriptions state that the Mannaeans, the Scythians under their king Ispakaia, and some tribes of the Zagros Mountains were a nuisance.

Following Ispakaia was King Bartatua who demanded the hand of Assyrian King Asarhaddon's daughter in marriage about 670 BC.

In 650 BC his son Madyes aligned with the Median Empire. Madyes conquered and ruled the Median Empire from about 633 to 625 BC.

Next came King Lycus about 630 who was followed by King Gnurus about 620 BC.

King Saulius 589 BC killed his own brother Anacharsis, an uncle of Idanthyrsus king of Scythia. Anacharsis left his country for Hellas and followed the customs of the Greeks.

King Skuka was defeated by Darius in about 520 BC. He is recorded by Darius on the Behistun Rock inscriptions as described later.

Across the Straits

In 513 BC, King Idanthyrsus retreats before Darius' army as noted earlier.

Herodotus describes King Scyles (500 BC) who suffered a similar fate as his great uncle Anacharsis. Scyles was the heir and son of the king Ariapeithes and a Greek woman from Istria. He was expelled by his people, and was executed by his brother.

King Ariapifa reigned in about 480 BC and was followed

by King Octamasadas in 450 BC who killed his own king brother Scyles and the Scythians took Octamasadas for their leader.

King Ateas who lived from 429 to 339 BC and was aged 90 fell in battle against Philip II of Macedonia in 339 BC near the Danube River. He was the most powerful king of Scythia whose name also occurs as Altheas, Ateia, Ataias, and Ateus.

King Scilurus (125 to 110 BC) died during a war against Mithridates VI of Pontus. He and his family are interred in the mausoleum in Neopolis Scythia, near Simferopol, in the Crimea.

Finally King Palacus (130 BC) was the last recorded Scythian ruler and was defeated by a commander of Mithridates VI of Pontus.

Both Teushpa and Tugdamme were known by the Assyrians and Babylonians as kings of the Umman-Manda or "large numerous horde".

Scythian Rule

After severing ties with the Cimmerians, the Assyrians welcomed the Scythians as allies and used them against the Medes and Egypt. This apparently took place in the latter half of the 7th century BC based on the Assyrian's first mentioning of the Cimmerians on stone inscriptions in 714 BC.

The Scythians ended up ruling western Asia for 28 years although they were in the region for many more decades. Eventually both the Cimmerian and Scythian tribes returned to the north where they merged with Celtic tribes who were also their cousins. Although, while in recorded history the Scythian period lasted a short time, they made an impact on history that lasted for more than a thousand years. In Europe north of the Black Sea however, the heartland and territories they dominated continued to be known as greater Scythia. They took part in the greatest campaigns of their times, defeating such mighty contemporaries as Assyria, Urartu, Babylonia, and Media.

The Scythians also came to terms with Egypt without having to fight. The Scythians engaged in distant wars. They didn't seek dominion for themselves, only glory, and, when victorious, declined to govern those whom they subdued.

Scythian Narrative I

The Wagon Leader was talking to the Scythian: "I don't know what we'd have done without you, and we're glad you came along. But you seem to be a dangerous man. The Scythian stared at him. "You didn't seem to mind my killing Cimmerians!" he said sarcastically. "In fact, you killed a few yourself!"

"Don't get me wrong!" The Wagon Leader persisted. "I'm not denying you helped us! Without you I don't know whether we could have beat off

those Cimmerians or not, but killing Cimmerians and killing our kind is a different thing!"

The Scythian's voice was rough. "You're new to the area. In a short time you'll find there are some men in this area that need to be killed more than Cimmerians."

The Scythian swung his horse around and moved off toward the hills. Inwardly, he was seething. He felt that he was a fool to stay on with the wagon train with his family. Not a man here liked him, none talked to him except of necessity. He wasn't even a member of their tribe, except by accident.

They had found him and his family at the crossing of the Araxes River. The Scythian was half dead with two arrow wounds in his body while his wife and children were ready to drop from fatigue.

His wife was able to bed him down in a spare wagon that was already carrying an old wounded man and was able to care for both of them.

Neither the Scythian nor his family offered an explanation of his wounds, and they talked little. He was a grim and lonely man, gentle words came hard and he could only look up into his wife's beautiful face lacking the words to convey his feelings.

His war battered body was too used to pain to remain helpless for long. He recovered rapidly, and afterwards rode along with the wagons, hunting for fresh meat and helping when he could.

He was not a man who made friends easily, yet gradually things improved, and the clannishness of the tribe's members was breaking down.

He often talked with his wife, riding beside the wagon, speaking of the mountains, their future, and his own former reckless and lonely life.

Their Migration Experiences

Chapter Three: Moving South Chasing the Cimmerians

As mentioned, when the Scythians encountered the Cimmerians in their old homelands north of the Black Sea, the Cimmerians took flight moving south across the Bosporus, through the city of Maykop, and across the Caucasus Mountain into north and east Anatolia.

The Bosporus

The eastern route around the Black Sea from Europe passed through the Crimea and south across the narrow strait that provides the opening to the Sea of Azov from the Black Sea. Today, it is known as the Kerch Strait and was formerly known as the Cimmerian Bosporus. The western route, known as the Bosporus strait, is a natural waterway that forms part of the boundary between Europe and Asia. The Asian and European sides of Istanbul is the only passage leading west into the Aegean and Mediterranean Seas from the Sea of Marmara and the Black Sea.

Maykop

In the course of many migrations traveling both north and south to skirt the eastern end of the Black Sea, the paths on the way to and from the Caucasus Mountains led through many small villages and the small city of Maykop.

The Caucasus passes

The ancient migration paths that earlier began in the Eurasian steppes and later spread back north, both east and west of the Caspian Sea. To the west as mentioned earlier, they moved into the Volga and Don River Valleys.

As noted, some moved south through a pass, which is today known as the Darial Pass and the Georgian Military Road in the Caucasus Mountains. This pass or gorge is alternatively known as the

Iberian Gates or the Caucasian Gates and in earlier times, this pass was allegedly known as *The Pass of Israel.*

Darial Gorge

The *Darial Pass* was historically important as the most direct passage across the Caucasus. It has been long fortified, at least since 150 BC. Ruins of an ancient fortress are still visible. The Russian fort, Darial, which guarded this section of the Georgian Military Road, was built at the northern end of the gorge

To the west of this route lay the Halys River where early migrations moving north and south from Europe and Asia met.

To the east on the shore of the Caspian Sea is another route mentioned earlier, the *Derbent Passage*, which was also used for trade but travelers may have been required to pay a higher fee for passage.

Derbent Passage

According to Herodotus, the Scythians came from the north side of the Black Sea through Derbent Passage to the South Caucasus and from there to Asia Minor in the 700s BC. Derbent is the southernmost city in Russia and claims to be the oldest. It is often identified with the Gates of Alexander and, since antiquity, it has been the eastern gate to the Caucasus. The city is located between two walls, stretching from the mountains to the sea that forms a passage about two miles wide.

It is also thought that some Jews from the Babylonian or Persian captivity moved across the Derbent Pass in the Caucasus to the lower Volga, since there are tombstones in that region bearing Jewish names, dating back to 157 BC and earlier.

Anatolia

As noted before, the route that some of the Cimmerians

took when they were forced out of the land north of the Black Sea by the Scythians, after passing south of the Caucasus', was west into Anatolia along the south shore of the Black Sea and into the Cappadocia area.

At the time of the Persian King Cyrus, the boundary between the Median and the Lydian empires was the river Halys. This stream, which rises in the mountain country of Armenia, runs first through Cilicia; afterwards it flows with the Matieni people on the right, and the Phrygians on the left. Then, it proceeds with a northern course, separating the Cappadocian Syrians from the Paphlagonian people, who occupy the left bank, thus forming the boundary of almost the whole of Lower Asia.

Gordium was the capital of ancient Phrygia. It was located a short distance southwest of Ankara, in the immediate vicinity of today's Polatli. The ancient city of Pessinus is nearby and it is said that here is where the mythological Phrygian King Midas was buried. It is also, where the ancient road between Lydia and Assyria and Babylonia crossed the river Sangarius (Sakarya River).

As noted earlier, the Scythian Tribe continued into Assyria along the western shore of the Caspian Sean while the Cimmerian tribes split into several groups with some settling in Sinope, some for a while in Gumrii, Georgia, and others continued toward Assyria.

Conflict North of Black Sea

As noted, the Scythians fell upon the Cimmerians so that part of them were destroyed, part were driven west and part to the southeast. Some of the Cimmerians, led by King Lygdames, fled along the same track in which the attack had come. They crossed the Caucasus Mountains through the Darial Gorge while the Scythians kept the Caucasus Mountains upon their right. The Scythians poured into Media via the Derbent Passage, in today's Azerbijian on the Caspian Sea. Current roads north of the Caucasus show how the combined movements could have taken place.

Scythian Narrative II

The Scythians left the Derbent Passage behind them and moved south. Their pace slowed, the horses moved step after step and the landscape before them seemed to go on forever. They stared un-seeing into the distance before them with nothing but repetitive ground to look at. There was nothing on which to focus.

With the Caspian Sea to the left and foothills to the right they increased the separation from the Cimmerians and their King Lygdames.

The Scythian scout mentioned earlier was riding away from the wagons alone. He drew in his horse and turned, glancing back at the long line. Some led horses and there were a few warrior outriders, yet none rode so far out as himself.

From where he sat he could not see their faces, but in the days past he had seen them many times, and the expression of each was engraved in his mind. Worn, hungry for rest and cool water, he knew that in the heart of each there was a longing to stop.

The Scythian had a wife and children as well as his horse, and weapons. He looked back to the last wagon where his wife with the red-gold hair sat on the driver's seat. In the back of that heavily loaded wagon were their boy and girl plus the older man who was restless with fever. He was nursing a wound in his thigh, a memento from battle with the Cimmerian warriors.

The earlier Scythian's wife's vision of future battles had finally come true.

While the Scythian tribe was chasing the Cimmerians, there was still the vision of distant hills and prosperous land sought by all wandering peoples. No hardship seemed too great. It was always the same when men envisioned a future opening beyond the hills, yet the vision must hold meaning and the end of the trail must bring reality since their women and children were either in the wagons or walking along side.

Past Derbent, the tribe soon turned inland away from the Caspian Sea and crossed the large river delta where the Araxes and Cyrus rivers merged. They settled on the far shore in the Kingdom of Urartu where some of them stayed for many generations while others continued south into Assyrian held lands.

When they were ready to stop, from the head of the train came a prolonged, yell as the wagon leader swung his arm in a great circle. The lead horse turned to swing in the beginning of the wagon circle.

The Scythian touched the horse with his heels and rode slowly toward the wagons. The leader's weariness and worry showed in his face. He said to the Scythian, "we're short on food and we need to keep all our horses and livestock. You seem to be the best hunter among us."

"All right," said the Scythian. "I'll go into the hills hunting and see what I can do, after my wife's wagon is in place, the camp is set up, and all their needs are met."

Future Conflicts

In the meantime, everyone knew that battles and conflict were ahead.

Over several decades after settling in Gyumri, the Cimmerians became involved in conflicts with the Scythians again, sometimes opposing one another, and at other times in concert against a common enemy.

At different times, both were mercenaries serving first under one ruler then another. They had developed relations with Urartu, Media, Assyria, and Babylon.

Some of the other Scythians returned to their abode south of the Caspian Sea and later co-ruled Media; and at another time, married into the Assyrian royal house.

Both tribes covered a lot of territory interacting with many other groups. Sometimes fighting and sometimes assimilating with others, including various captives of the Assyrians.

The Nomads

Their Migration Experiences

Chapter Four: Campaigns in Anatolia, Assyria, and Babylon

King Rusa

The Cimmerians helped the Assyrians defeat Urartu in 714 BC, then Urartu chose to submit to the Assyrians, and together the two defeated the Cimmerians. Gamir is first mentioned in a military intelligence report to King Sargon II concerning campaigns in Urartu. It is in the form of a letter, which states that King Rusa I of Urartu marched his troops to Gamir, land of the Cimmerians, but was defeated. Another name may be Gyumri.

An official record in city of Gyumri in Georgia states that the city's name came from the Cimmerians.

In central Georgia, archeologists also have found the greatest concentration of materials of the Scythian type, with the earliest dating to about 700 BC.

King Sargon

Sargon II reigned for seventeen years from 722 to 705 BC. He led campaigns against Urartu and the Medes, annexed numerous states in Syria and southern Anatolia, defeated the Aramaeans in the central Tigris Valley, and the Chaldeans in the lower Euphrates Valley.

In order to ensure effective control of this vast empire, extending from the border of Egypt to the Zagros Mountains and from the Taurus Mountains to the Persian Gulf, Sargon divided it into some 70 provinces, each headed by a governor who was directly responsible to the king.

In his capital, Calah, he created a central administrative organization and delegated some of his own power to his son Sennacherib who reigned from 705 to 681 BC.

There were many conquests and deportations by Sargon II. In an inscription, Sargon states that he besieged and conquered the Northern Israelite Kingdom's capital city of Samaria. He said, "I took as booty 27,290 people who lived there. I gathered 50 chariots from them. I taught the rest (of the deportees) their skills."

He also boasts that he repopulated Samaria after deporting its Israelite inhabitants. Assyrian records reveal that Israelite deportees served as military personnel, officials, priests, skilled laborers and merchants. Israelites in these roles were normally treated as Assyrian subjects.

According to Assyrian military intelligence reports to Sargon recorded on clay tablets found in the Royal Archives of Nineveh by Sir Henry Layard, the Cimmerians invaded Urartu from Mannai in 714 BC. From there they turned west along the coast of the Black Sea as far as Sinope, visiting with some tribal family members and friends, and then headed south in Anatolia towards Tabal, a vassal state of Assyria, defeating an Assyrian army in central Anatolia, that resulted in Sargon II's death in 705.

Accounts of Sargon II written during his reign highlight his victory over his northern neighbors, tells of the Urartians, and the looting of their sanctuaries in 714 BC.

About 715 BC a Median chieftain, led the Medes in an unsuccessful rebellion against the Assyrian king Sargon II.

Manda and Umman-Manda

The name Manda in the Babylonian text applies to the same people that were called Sakae or (Sacae) Scythians by the Greeks. The term Umman-Manda is a general designation for nomadic northmen (Umman - a horde; Manda - full, numerous). There are several references to the Umman-Manda as being Cimmerian and Scythian. Both Tugdamme and Tueshpa appear in a prayer from Ashurbanipal to Marduk, on a fragment at the British Museum as king of the Umman-Manda.

King Sennacherib

Sometime between 620 and 617 BC Nebuchadnezzar, King of Babylon, made an alliance with Media that was formally sealed by the marriage between Cyaxares' daughter Amytis and Nebuchadnezzar's son. Thus, Cyaxares' son Astyages, King of the Medes, became brother-in-law of Nebuchadnezzar.

During the reign of Sennacherib, whose father was Assyria's Sargon II, Babylonia was in a constant state of revolt that ended with the complete destruction of the city in 689 BC. Sennacherib used Cimmerian mercenaries in the action. He razed the entire city and, despite its traditional status as a holy city, he flooded the site. Its walls, temples and palaces were razed, and the rubble was thrown into the sea, which at that time was near

Babylon. His son, Esarhaddon rebuilt the old city and made it his part-time residence.

King Esarhaddon

Esarhaddon's son, Assurbanipal, was the last strong king of the Assyrian Empire from about 668 to 627 BC. The Babylonians, in coalition with the Medes and Scythians, defeated the Assyrians in 612 BC and sacked Nimrud and Nineveh. Assurbanipal later reclaimed Babylon but in a subsequent overthrow of the Assyrian Empire, the Babylonians reclaimed control.

During the early seventh century BC, conditions on the northeast frontier of Assyria were unsteady, as was indicated by the queries of Esarhaddon addressed to the sun-god Shamash. One text mentions a great coalition of Mannaeans, Cimmerians, and Medes against Assyria headed by Phraortes, the Median king. Esarhaddon warded off the danger by making friends with the Scythians.

As a result, Phraortes was defeated in 674 BC, and the coalition disintegrated. He was later killed by the Scythians in 653 BC. A Scythian incursion into Urartu resulted in a considerable loss of Urartian territory in the south east. Subsequently Urartu was subdued by Scythians, and soon afterwards, about 652 BC, the countries of Mannaea and Media were subjugated.

Assyrian records of the seventh century BC mention the Cimmerians in connection with wars and unrests. After their first recorded encounter with the Urartians, they probably split into two groups, of which one moved westward and the other went south eastwards, along Lake Urmia.

Assyrian religious texts of the time of Esarhaddon mention the Cimmerians in the region of Lake Urmia and their alliance with the Medes. Sulimirski and Taylor state that several scholars believe that a section of these Cimmerians proceeding further south reached Luristan, and that they were responsible for the introduction of a series of bronze articles. They were part of the Koban culture and the Luristan bronze industry of the eighth to seventh centuries BC."

King Assurbanipal

Assurbanipal is famed for amassing a significant collection of cuneiform documents in his royal palace at Nineveh. This collection, known as the Library of Ashurbanipal, is now housed at the British Museum.

Babylon had captured and exiled the Kingdom of Judah in 586 BC. The prophet Jeremiah had prophesied the exile of the Jews and the expected destruction of Babylonia by the Scythians (Ashkenaz), and kingdoms of Ararat, Media, and Minni. This didn't take place however - the Neo-Babylonian Empire fell to Cyrus the Great, king of Persia in 539 BC who in 536 BC allowed the exiled Jews to return to Judah and rebuild the Temple, which was completed in the sixth year of Darius' reign in 515 BC.

Several centuries later Persia's Babylon fell to Alexander the Great.

The Persian Empire was a series of successive empires that ruled over the Iranian plateau, the original Iranian homeland, and beyond in Western Asia, South Asia, Central Asia and the Caucasus. The first Persian Empire was formed under the Median Empire, which lasted from about 728 to 559 BC.

The Persian Empire came into being after the Medes defeated and ended the Assyrian Empire with the help of Babylonians and others.

Median Kings

In the time of Assyria's kings Sargon II and Esarhaddon, the Cimmerians operated mainly from the Zagros Mountains and from Media. Their area extended from Mannae in the north to Ellipi or Elam in the south and included parts of Media proper in the east. *The Fortresses of Mannae* were in the Cimmerians area as well as where some of the captives were deported.

The major Median city of Ecbatana (Hamadan), which according to the Bible, was also one of the "cities of the Medes" to which the exiled Assyrian captives were taken, appears to have once been controlled by Daiaukku.

When the Median tribes intermittently came under control of Assyria *Daiaukku*, a Mannaean governor, had been responsible to the Assyrians for Cimmerian held fortresses in the region. Daiaukku had plotted with Urartu against Assyria and was exiled by the Assyrians to Hamath.

In about 675 BC, the Assyrian land of Hamadan (Ecbatana) was surrounded by the Medians and taken by the Median chief Phraortes with the help of the Cimmerians.

This is close to Takab, *The Throne of Solomon*, an archaeological site that lies midway between Urmia and Hamadan. At the same time, some Scythians were laying siege to Bit-Kari, southeast of Hamadan.

Phraortes, who reigned from 675 to 633 BC united the Median tribes and expelled the Assyrians. He was killed by the Scythians, who had invaded Media from the northwest and ruled until 625 BC. Phraortes son, Cyaxares gained back the kingdom and reigned from 625 to 585 BC. He chose as his capital the city of Ecbatana today's Hamadan in Iran.

In 626 BC, as noted above, when Assyria was in turmoil and menaced by the Medes, Scythians, and Cimmerians, Nebuchadnezzar proclaimed himself king of Babylonia in 625 and allied himself with the Medes to help destroy Assyrian might.

In approximately 625 BC, the Scythians are in Media and the Medes and Babylonians begin to assert their independence from Assyria and attack Nineveh .

Prior to the death of Ashurbanipal two Median invasions of Assyria had taken place: one under Phraortes about 634 BC, which was defeated. The second was under Cyaxares who had besieged Nineveh with allies and the Scythians under King Madyes came later to seal Assyria's defeat.

Herodotus states "A battle was fought, in which the Assyrians suffered a defeat, and Cyaxares had already begun the siege of the place, when a numerous horde of Scythians, under their king Madyes burst into Asia in pursuit of the

Cimmerians whom they had driven out of Europe earlier, and entered the Median territory."

As noted above, Phraortes was killed in a battle against Ashurbanipal, the king of Assyria. After his fall, the Scythians took over. Later, Cyaxares, seeking revenge, killed some of the Scythian leaders and proclaimed himself as King of Medes. Cyaxares then joined with King Nebuchadnezzar of Babylonia and befriended the Scythian King Madyes.

The Babylonian alliance was formalized through the marriage of Cyaxares daughter, Amytis with Nebuchadnezzar's son, Nebuchadnezzar II, the king who constructed the Hanging Gardens of Babylon as a present for his Median wife to help with her homesickness for the mountainous country of her birth. These allies, along with Scythians, overthrew the Assyrian Empire and destroyed Nineveh in 612 BC.

In 591 BC, Cyaxares attacked Lydia in western Anatolia. In order to be absolutely certain that there was no danger to his army from behind, he placed a regiment of Median soldiers under the leadership of Madyes, the son of Bartatua who had helped him with his Scythian hordes in the destruction of the Assyrian capital Nineveh. It appears the intention of Cyaxares was to subdue Urartu and remove any threat to his campaign.

Madyes with his horde of Scythians combined with the small army of the Medians succeeded to overrun most of Urartu and devastated the main cities, which has been verified by archaeological exploration.

For several years, Alyattes II, king of Lydia from 619 to 560 BC, was considered to be the founder of the Lydian empire. He continued the war against Miletus begun by his father, but was obliged to turn his attention towards the Medes and Babylonians, which is discussed later.

In 585 BC, the Kingdom of Urartu suffers following the Median invasion. The Medes overran the Urartian state then fought a battle with the Lydians who had come to dominate West Central Anatolia.

Alyattes II's power extended to the river Halys which was designated the frontier between the two powers in Asia Minor. The kings of Babylonia and Kilikia (Cilicia) both helped draw up the peace, but the Urartians did not take part in the negotiations and no longer appear to have been a power in the East.

Allattes II also conquered the Ionian cities of Smyrna (now Izmir) and Colophon. His tomb, one of the wonders of antiquity, is located near the river Hermus (modern Gediz), north of Sardis. His son, Croesus, was the last king of Lydia.

Astyages had succeeded his father Cyaxares in 585 BC, following the Battle of Halys, which ended a five-year war between the Lydians and the Medes. He inherited a large empire, ruled in alliance with his two king brothers-in-law, Croesus of Lydia and Nebuchadnezzar of Babylon.

Cyaxares has been referred to as King of Umman-Manda. In regard to the Medes or Cimmerians who advanced against Cyrus, Astyages is also mentioned as king of the Umman-Manda. In about 550 BC, Astyages' army mutinied, the king was captured and he was handed over to Cyrus.

King Midas

By from about 725 to 675 BC, the Phrygian empire had developed into a regional power, under King Midas, with its capital at Gordion. The stability of the area was undermined by the conflicts between Assyria and Urartu and by the incursions of Cimmerians and Scythians from the Pontic Steppe in the eighth and seventh century BC. During this period, Gordion was destroyed by Cimmerians and the power of the Phrygians collapsed.

Lydia's King Madys

The Cimmerians overran Asia Minor, plundered Sardis, destroyed Magnesia (near Miletus on the Meander River), and defeated the empire of Lydia as well as Ephesus.

Tueshpa, the leader of the Gimirrai, is called a Manda by Esarhaddon as stated earlier.

Tueshpa's first known attacks were against the Greek coastal cities in Asia Minor. In 653 BC, he began to push at the mighty Assyrian Empire during the reign of Ashurbanipal.

An inscription of Assurbanipal returns thanks to the Assyrian gods for the defeat of Tueshpa of the Manda who led the Cimmerians into Kalikia

(Cilicia), from thence they afterwards marched westward and burned Sardis.

Herodotus states that on May 28, 585 BC, the Lydians were at war with the Medes, a remnant of the first wave of Cimmerians in the region, over the issue of refuge the Lydians had given to some Scythian soldiers of fortune that were hostile to the Medes. The war endured for five years, but in the sixth, an eclipse of the sun spontaneously halted the Battle of Halys progress. The Battle was a war fought by the Lydians against Cyaxares, king of Media and based on the solar eclipse, the Lydians and Medes made peace immediately, swearing a blood oath.

Both the Cimmerians and Scythians were Nomads, they could also be termed Umman-Manda. It is easy to see how different writers became confused at times as to who was who.

During the chase of the Scythians after the Cimmerians through the Caucasus Mountains, Some of the Scythians stayed behind in a place called Saka. They lived there many years, however a longing for departed family members caused some individual families to travel on.

Bru's Narrative

An example follows of how one Scythian family survived as they traveled from Saka, through Urartu and Assyria to where family members had migrated to Anatolia's land of Lydia.

From Saka, they traveled north of Lake Van skirting the shore and on into the Musair region. They had stopped for a rest in Assyria before continuing on towards Phrygia and Lydia.

The Cimmerians had been very active in Assyria, Anatolia and Media. At one time they were both friends and mercenaries for the Assyrians and at another time they were enemies. The King of the Cimmerians, Tueshpa, was well known by the Assyrians and the local people and for the time being their abode in Musair was known as Cimmerian country.

They had to be cautious now since they were in Cimmerian country. They were distant cousins to the Cimmerians, plus the fact that they were traveling alone, made them feel safe as long as they kept to themselves and didn't gossip with the locals.

After crossing a river, they stopped at a small settlement north of the village of Musair.

When Bru's wife, Sun, stepped down from the wagon near the settlement, her husband had the fire going but he sat, forearms resting on his knees, hands hanging loose, staring into the flames.

"Bru?" Sun was a slender, graceful and unusually pretty woman. "Bru? What is it?" He said "It's this... all of it." The Scythian, Bru's gesture took in their surroundings. "I had no right to bring you and our boy into this, no right at all."

"We discussed it Bru. We all took part in the decision. We all decided it was the best thing to move where our relatives have migrated." "I know Sun, but that was earlier. It was one thing to sit in a comfortable place and talk about what could be better, but it's something else when you are face to face with it." He looked, toward the open plains. "What's out there Sun? What are we getting into?"

Brun was twelve and came running. "Somebody's coming Dad." His father may have had doubts, but Brun had none. His parents looked where he pointed. A rider was coming through the scattered trees toward them. He was a tall rough-looking man on a big horse, and he carried his weapons as though they were a part of him. He pulled up some fifty yards off. His eyes swept

the camp and he said "Hello. All right if I come in?"

There was nothing about his looks to inspire confidence but Bru said, "It's all right. Come on in. "The person rode up, stopping across the fire from their wagon, dismounting with his horse between himself and the fire.

The person was actually a Cimmerian who had been exiled from his tribe. His mother was an Assyrian captive, a Northern Kingdom Israelite, from Samaria and his father was a Cimmerian. His mother had named him after her Samarian father, Yau.

His family had been unable to assimilate and he was an outcast, but they were somewhat distant cousins and looked like one of them. He seemed to be ok.

The Person said "My name is Yau … I saw the smoke from your fire., and thought you might be willing to share a meal. He walked to the fire, seeing

Sun he removed his hat. "Sorry woman. I don't want to intrude but I've been riding all night, and have had little to eat or drink for several days. "She said "I'm sorry too. This morning's meal will be ready soon."

Bru introduced himself and said "This is my wife Sun, and this is my son Brun." Yau said "Good to meet you both."

He added a stick to the fire, glancing at the wagon and the deep-cut tracks and said. "You have a heavy load in your wagon. You aren't going too far, I hope."

Bru said "We're going west to where our relatives have migrated," "You aren't going far with that load" Yau said.

He accepted the cup of broth Sun poured for him and sat on the wagon tongue. "You've got four good looking horses pulling the wagon, but that's too much load."

"We'll manage," Bru's tone was cool. Yau was, Sun decided, good looking in a rough way.

Like most men, he was bearded; his clothes were shabby, yet there was an animal strength about him and an almost a cat-like grace.

Yau said "this is a good drink." He reached for the hot vessel and refilled his cup. He said "Ever driven on the ground beyond here?" Bru said "I've driven on similar ground."

Yau said "It looks like rain. The grass is good for the stock, but soft ground from a rain makes the pulling mighty hard. You aren't going far with just four horses and a load that heavy. And supposing your horses wander off? How'll you find them?" Bru said "We have horses we can ride."

Yau sipped his hot drink. "Not anymore. They're gone." Bru said "What's that?" Yau said "You had a pair of big brown horses, right?"

Bru said "Yes." Yau said "They're gone. Some men took them."

"What?" Bru came to his feet. "What do you mean?" Yau said "A couple of Cimmerians drove them off just before full light. Men from the settlement, over there."

Bru said "I don't think they stole them." Sun said to her son "Brun, you better go and check on the horses."

Sun was slicing meat into a metal pan, her face flushed from the heat. Yau said "You are a beautiful woman." She said "Thank you, but don't get any wrong ideas."

Yau asked "When you crossed the river, back there you came right up through the settlement of wagons, didn't you?" Bru did not like this man and said. "We stopped there."

Yau said "I knew you had. They saw your stock, and they saw your wife."

Bru said "What do you mean by that?" Yau said "There are some mean Cimmerians in the settlement. You probably saw only the good ones. There are mean people who saw your heavy-loaded wagon, your wife, and your stock and are planning to take it all."

Brun came running, his face white. "Dad! The horses are gone! Their tracks lead right toward the settlement."

Bru felt sick. He had known there might be trouble in coming west, but felt sure that if he minded his own business he could stay out of it. He got up slowly, then went to the wagon for his bow, arrows, and sword.

"Bru?" Sun was frightened and Bru said "I have to get those horses. I'll go over and hopefully, I can bring them back."

Yau picked two slices of meat from the hot pan. Without looking up he said, "You ever kill a man, Bru?" "Kill a man?" Bru was startled. "Only a few in battle."

Yau said "If you walk into that settlement with weapons, you better figure on using them." Bru said "I don't think-"

and Yau said "You walk into that place without being ready to kill and your wife will be a widow before the hour is up."

Bru said "I can use these weapons. I've killed a dozen deer with this bow and arrows." Yau said "Were they launching arrows back at you?" He said "They plan on you coming over." "They want you to. Why do you suppose they left all the tracks? They figure to kill you." They've seen your woman. They figure your stock and your wagon load are worth something. They took your horses and know you will come looking for them. They want you to come armed. They will say you've made a fight, so they just had to kill you."

Bru said "So what am I to do? Let them steal my horses?" Yau said "No, you just go in there with your eyes open, thinking you are going to kill somebody. You spot one of them, preferably a big man, and when you start talking, you just

sort of careless-like have your arrow cocked and pointed at him. Then you tell them to bring out your horses."

Sun said "Bru? Don't do it. It isn't worth it. Not for two horses." Bru said "We raised those horses Sun, and they belong to us. I shall go after them."

Yau said "He's got to try ma'am. If he doesn't go in they will steal your wagon and the other horses."

"How do you know so much about it?" Sun demanded "How do we know you are not one of them?" Yau grinned and was amused. "You don't."

Bru said, again. "I'm going," Yau said "You better while your courage is up. You just go right on in, and don't you worry about your wife or son, if anything happens to you, I'll take care of them."

Bru said "Now, see here!" Yau said "You have to do it and better get started."

Bru hesitated, glancing from one to the other. "Bru," Sun said quietly, "if it must be done, do it, and don't worry about me. I will be all right."

Brun said "Dad? Can I go with you? I can handle a bow and arrow too!" Bru said "You stay with your mother."

Bru took up his weapons and walked toward the settlement. His mouth was dry and he was frightened. There were only three hundred yards to the settlement, and he did not know whether he wished it were nearer or farther. He had seen the men sitting around the wagons as he and his family drove through the group and he had been glad to leave them behind.

He thought of his Bow. It was a good one, and he could launch an arrow straight, but he had never released an arrow at a man except in battle. Could he do it now? And that Yau who he had left his wife and son with. How did he know that the man was not worse than any of those in the settlement?

The settlement was there, right in front of him. The horses were there too, tied to one of the wagons. No attempt had been made to conceal them. They were a challenge, and a clear affront to him.

He remembered how those men had looked at Sun. He had planned to leave earlier, but he had hesitated, for once they left the river and its rim of trees, they began to talk about all they left behind. Their travel had only been a topic of conversation until they actually packed up and started on their journey.

Men were waiting for him at the settlement. He could see two men seated on a rough plank, another standing by a wagon and they had seen him coming. He could not turn back now. They would know he was afraid.

Yau was right. They planned to kill him. How? It was all so obvious.

The horses were there, he had only to walk in, state his ownership and bring them away. That was all... or was it?

Back at the fire Yau emptied his cup. Sun's features were white and strained. "Well," Yau said, "you better make your plans. I wouldn't give your husband a chance in Hell. You're very likely going to be a widow. Now I'm not much, but-"

Sun said "You're going to let him be killed?" Yau said "It's none of my affair." She said "Help him." He said "You are his woman?" She said "We are married." He said "That wasn't what I asked. I wanted to know if you were really his woman. It isn't always the same thing." She said "I am his woman and am proud to be so. He is a fine man. And I am a decent woman."

Of course, if he gets himself killed, you have a choice... me or them." Sun replied. "I shall go back home. I am sure Brun and I could get along." Lazily, he got to his feet and moved to his horse, and said "I'll just head on over and see the fun." He swung on to the horse. "

Yau grinned at her and turned his horse. As soon as he emerged from the trees he could see Bru walking into the settlement. Yau turned his horse to use the cover of the trees and came up at an angle from which he could not be seen as he watched Bru. Drawing up in the shade of the trees, he drew his bow and an arrow from its scabbard. There really was not much he could do. So much would depend on how the game was played.

Yau could hear Bru speaking. "I see you found my horses. Thank you for holding them for me."

The thin man who answered him seemed amused. "Your horses, you say? Now how would we know that? Those horses came wandering in, and my son tied them up. We figure to keep them." Bru said "The horses belong to me." The man grinned lazily, a taunting grin. "I don't believe it nor do any of my friends."

Bru remembered what Yau had said. A big man was lounging against a wagon. Bru shifted his feet slightly, and managed to point the bow and cocked arrow at the big man as he turned in an easy, natural movement, and suddenly it was covering the big man.

Bru said "I'll take my horses. I am sure you will thank your son for me, but tell your friends that we raised these horses and we're going to keep them."

He stepped toward the horses. The thin man spat and said "If you untie those horses somebody might get the wrong idea. Are you ready to die?"

Bru kept his eyes on the big man as he spoke to the thin one. "Even if you were to launch an arrow at me, I would still release the arrow from this bow and I couldn't miss that big man standing by the wagon." The bow didn't move – his left hand held his bow with a finger wrapped around the arrow drawn tight, still aimed at the big man. Bru was able to untie the rope holding their horses with his right hand.

The big man said "Don't anybody be foolish! Give him the horses. Let them go!"

Holding the bow steady, Bru put a foot up on the bench and swung on to the horse. Turning his horse he untied the second horse, keeping his bow in position as he did so. He backed the horses into the street, keeping the bow and arrow pointed at the big man, but as he turned the horses his bow swung off target and in an instant the big man disappeared behind the wagon, the other men threw themselves right and left disappearing.

Bru saw and heard Arrows being launched!, and in an instant of stark panic he realized he had been perfectly set up, the horses and the men around the wagons were drawing his full attention while Yau was behind him.

He heard the whistle of an arrow past his cheek and turning quickly saw two more arrows. He sharply turned his horse to look back.

Everyone had disappeared, but from the rear opening of a wagon hung the body of a man, his head and one arm visible.

In the shadow of the trees near the entrance to the settlement, there was Yau, holding a bow in his hand.

Yau said "You're ok! Just back off easy now, and if you see anything move, put an arrow in it."

With his loaded and drawn bow, Bru rode diagonally away from the settlement, keeping his bow and arrow on target.

Turning sharply then, he trotted his horse away under cover of the trees.

Suddenly Bru was shaking all over, and his stomach felt empty and sick.

Later he told his family "It was Yau who put the arrow into the man in the back of the wagon, but I couldn't thank him … he already left!"

Their Migration Experiences

Chapter Five: Assimilating Israelites, Cimmerians, and Scythians

The Israelite Captives

Tiglath-Pileser III's terrifying army attacked Northern Israel in 734 BC. The victorious king then deported "the Reubenites, the Gadites and half of the Manasseh's tribe" to Assyria. He was the first Assyrian king to oversee a deportation of Israelites and claimed to have taken 13,520 captives from Lower Galilee alone.

A second invasion of the Northern Kingdom took place at the capital city of Samaria by Assyria's King Sargon II in about 721 BC. As mentioned earlier, he exiled about 22,000 captives from the Northern Kingdom, and moved the them to various cities in Assyria. He then brought previous captives from earlier campaigns into Samaria to assure that the land was kept productive.

Those that were exported were not held captive long but were free to assimilate, hold government jobs, engage in business, travel, etc. They were located into areas that included Assyrians, Cimmerians, and Scythians. There was plenty of opportunity to assimilate. The problem was that all three groups mentioned above were warlike peoples and were interested in fighting, conquests, and booty.

One of the Israelite Tribes carried away was the Tribe of Naphtali. Tobit, a northern Israelite deportee, is spoken of in the Bible's Book of Tobit "when he was made captive in the days of Sargon II. He became a captive in 721 BC and was deported and lived in the city of Nineveh in the seventh century BC. In his own account, he says that he was brought along with the tribe of Naphtali into captivity and he talks about being able to travel to other places in Assyria and in Media like Ecbatana and Rages near to today's Tehran.

The captives were also able to work in various jobs as artisans, laborers, soldiers, and government administrators.

The Bible states that the Israelites who were defeated by the Assyrians and were forcibly deported from their homeland and were relocated "in Halah, on the Habor, the river of Gozan, and in the cities of the Medes". Media is not far from the region of Urartu and is south of Lake Urmia and the Caspian Sea. Since Media was not controlled by Assyria until about a decade later, it may be that the deportation was only to cities on the border with Media or that it was a staged deportation that took place over 10 to 15 years.

As mentioned, the deported tribes were not necessarily treated as slaves in captivity. From the stories of Tobit, the Israelite, and Assyrian leaders' it is evident that they had freedom of movement. The distances in Assyria, Media, and Transcaucasia are not great and it was fairly easy to move from one part of a region to another.

Following their victory over the northern kingdom, the Assyrians soon returned in 701 BC, to attack the southern kingdom of Judah. Led by King Sennacherib, they captured most of Judah's fortified cities and deported thousands of their inhabitants. Jerusalem survived this invasion and they recovered sufficiently to last another 115 years until Jerusalem was conquered, destroyed, and it's people exiled to Babylon in 586 BC by the armies of Nebuchadnezzar.

The Mercenaries

During the reign of Sennacherib of Assyria, Babylonia was in a constant state of revolt and was suppressed only by the complete destruction of the city in 689 BC. Sennacherib used

Cimmerians in his army as mercenaries. As noted, an Assyrian document of 679 BC refers to an Assyrian commander of the Cimmerian regiment. In another Assyrian document however the Cimmerians are called the seed of runaways who know neither vows to the gods nor oaths.

The Cimmerians defeated Urartu somewhere between 714 and 707 BC. Since many Israelites were conscripted into the Assyrian Army, they were likely involved with fighting between Assyria and Urartu as well as her ally Minnai during the years 719 to 714 BC.

The religious texts of Esarhaddon about 673 BC verify that the Urartu King Rusa the Second recruited a large contingent of Cimmerians as mercenaries and a document of 672 BC mentions Urartu invasion of Phrygia in which Cimmerians participated.

The following example describes what life might have been like in that arid land.

Brun's Narrative

The four Scythian men lay in a flat place, pinned down by Cimmerian Mercenaries hired by Assyria during the invasion of Anatolia by Urartu and their Mercenaries.

The sun was high, two days had passed without water, four days without food, and they were down to only a few arrows left.

Before them was a peak they believed to be the main southeastern foothill of Mount Ararat; if so, there was a water source up a canyon to the right. Of this they could not be sure, but they believed in it as a dying man believes in God.

For three days they had thought of that water, longed for it, they dreamt wild dreams of it.

The most beautiful woman would have been traded by any one of them for a swallow of

57

water, even if it were brackish and smelled like skunk.

Earlier they were part of a patrol that left one of the *Mannae Fortresses* with six Scythian warriors and one leader. The leader was a proud, honorable, and decent young man with his first command, his first patrol into Cimmerian held country, where they had seen no enemies for two whole days and nights.

A camping spot had been decided upon, and when their guide advised against it the leader felt he could not permit his decision to be questioned. A short distance ahead, the guide assured him, there was a water source and a defensible position. The young leader hesitated, then decided to stay where they were.

They bedded down on level ground, in soft sand. The men slept well, for they were tired. Brun was to stand watch the first few hours, to be relieved by Astortes.

The night was very clear, and as always in arid land it was cool, almost cold. The heat of the day vanished with the sun, for the rocks and sand did not hold the heat, but gave it up quickly in the cold night air.

Brun was wary. He was an experienced warrior, he did not like the feel of the night, and had been watching the guide. The eastern Kurd came of a tribe that numbered great warriors among them, but they had been driven from their homeland and were now scattered widely over Assyria and Media. The guide had seemed uneasy, his head constantly turning, watching.

The attack came with the first light. Their horses were stampeded, one man was killed, another wounded. Although their warriors got off a few arrows, there was no indication they had hit anything. The Cimmerians vanished as they had come, fading into the sands like ghosts.

What followed was sheer hell. After waiting until the sun was up, the leader formed his warriors into a column and they started out. The leader walked beside Brun. "Well, they got what they wanted," he commented, "but it is good to be rid of them." Brun said "If we are!" The leader said "You don't think they have gone?" Then Brun said "No!" And the leader wanted to know "Then why don't they attack?"

Brun shrugged. "It is not their way. They are watching us from out there to see what we will do. They know this land having worked for the Assyrians. They know what is ahead and we do not. They can plan, but our reaction must depend on circumstances."

The leader said "You have had good training." "I'm educated and have a lot of experience" said Brun.

The leader glanced at him, but was silent. They plodded on through soft ground. The wounded man kept up. He had been fighting Cimmerians for a long time, and he knew what it would mean to fall behind.

The heat was stifling, and there were no clouds. Rocky ridges, with sparse vegetation, lay to the left and right. Occasionally there were scattered clusters of rock and more sparse vegetation.

At noon the leader called a brief halt. They ate a little dried meat and a few pieces of bread, and took a swallow of water.

"Sir?" "What is it Brun?"

"There's a long stretch of sand ahead and wide-open country. Off on the right there are some rocks. I suggest that we take shelter there until the sun goes down. I believe they plan to surround us out in the open, where the sun can do their work for them."

The idea appealed to the leader, and he had already ignored one bit of advice to their cost. "All right," he said, "until the sun goes down. We will march farther and faster, when it is cool."

Their approach to the rocks was wary, but they arrived safely. The open area's rocks were dark, a site not likely to be chosen by the Cimmerians who preferred a place under cover that could be easily held and still have a view of that area.

Once in the shade, the men sat down, removed their gear, and rested. The leader started to take a drink, then saw that the others didn't do so. Reluctantly he put his water container down, for he could not permit them to think he had less endurance than they had.

Brun watched the country around them, but the surrounding land showed nothing. The guide, a soft-walking man, came up beside him. "The leader listened to you," he said. "I hope he will continue to do so."

Brun said "Do you know where we are?" The guide replied and pointed "It looks like the southeast foothill of Mount Ararat. I'm not sure, but I think it's the right foothill." Brun said "You speak our languages well."

The guide said "I went to a good school for five years where I studied both Akkadian and Iranian languages plus I do listen." He said "I also worked in Tabriz with several Assyrian officers."

They did not talk any more, for their mouths were dry. The water in their containers would soon be gone, and Mount Ararat lay far off on the horizon.

With the first coolness, they started on. Occasionally the soft soil gave way to a harder surface, sometimes to scattered rocks over a hard-packed dirt and gravel surface.

Refreshed by their rest and by the coolness of the air, the men moved well. When an hour had passed and darkness was closing down on them, some had begun to straggle. The leader paused. "Close up now!" he said. He spoke quietly, but his voice carried. He said "Close it up"

After a while, they took a short break. The stars appeared, and they walked on, guided by them.

"The Cimmerians are like the Assyrians," the guide said. "They do not like to fight at night. The Medes however, like it better at night."

Wary of the rock walls now closing in, they made dry camp. The guide scouted for water, but found none. They slept fitfully through the night until the sky grew gray. Brun was the first man awake, in time to see a Cimmerian slipping from one rock to another.

Brun touched the leader and said, "They are closing in."

The last few stars still hung in the sky, and it was still cool. "We can move out," the leader said "All right, men, let's go."

They started, and for some reason no arrows were launched. Brun looked toward the horizon. It was going to be a brutal day.

An hour ... two hours. Ahead of them lay an apparently wide-open area of sand and scattered brush. Occasionally they saw a forest.

Another hour ... Every yard covered was to their advantage, but the Cimmerians were out there, and the Cimmerians knew how long it had been since the Scythians had stopped at a water source. They knew how little water the Scythians must have left, and they would know about the wounded man.

The Fort was three days' ride to the southeast. On foot, and under good conditions, it was four to five days, but without adequate water, they may last a day or two followed by death.

When the attack came it was completely unexpected. It came from a cluster of scattered low rocks that seemed to offer no substantial cover.

The first arrow caught the leader in the chest and he fell to the side. Automatically every man dropped to a knee and returned arrows.

The Cimmerians had vanished.

"They got my water container," the man named Astortes said. "They put a hole in it!"

"The guide said "I think that's what they wanted to do."

Brun held a container to the leader's lips, but he brushed it away. "You will need that Brun. You are in command now." He put a hand out to the guide. "I am sorry. I was wrong not to listen to you."

Brun looked around slowly, studying the terrain. There was nothing he could do for the leader. Even if they had been at the Fort, he would have died. Brun knew by the color of the blood and the froth on his lips. The arrow, of heavy shaft, had gone in under his left arm and through his lungs, cutting an artery in transit. He knew the leader was going to die, and the leader knew it too. He died quickly.

The guide crawled up beside Brun. "They have gone, I think. They want to kill us all, but they don't want to lose one of their own." Brun said "We have four water containers and five men. We will need water before anything else."

They rolled the body of the dead leader into a shallow place and covered the hastily made grave with rocks and soil. Brun mentally took note of what landmarks there were, and they continued on. No arrows came, no Cimmerian appeared.

Brun now had the leader's bow and thirty-two arrows. He had also taken his money, and whatever else was of value. These must be returned to the Fort, not only so the leader's relatives might have them, but so the Cimmerians might not get them.

The sun appeared over the mountains, and already they could feel its heat. Brun mentally measured the distance to the mountain toward which they were headed. It was far, much too far.

The surface was firm for a change. There were scattered, fist-sized rocks, and there was more brush, but none of it was more than knee-high. He led the way, holding his stride to easy measured steps. There was no cover near them now, neither shelter for an enemy nor for themselves.

Suddenly Brun saw two Cimmerian riders off to the left. He recognized his own horse, and swore softly. On the other side were two more Cimmerian riders, who made no attempt to draw closer. They didn't launch any arrows and remained well beyond range.

At mid-day Brun stopped the men in the middle of a broad open area. They were ready to drop with weariness.

He nodded off to their right. "See that bunch of rocks?" he said "We can make them by noon, and we can find shade there, enough to sit out the day."

Nobody spoke. Their faces showed their extreme fatigue. The wounded man, was bearing up well. Brun went to him. "Don't worry" the man said" when you get there, I'll be with you."

They ran, and for men half-dead from heat, exhaustion, and thirst, they ran well. Each man knew it was his own life that was at stake, his own life for which he ran. Arrows rained from the air, a man stumbled, ran on then fell. The guide was about to stop but Brun waved him on "Into the rocks!" he commanded.

He dropped to a knee, aimed at a rider, and let loose an arrow. The Cimmerian pulled up sharply, swung his horse and leaned over the opposite side for protection.

The others veered off, and he walked to their fallen man. It was Astortes, and he was dead.

Stripping him of his arrows, bow and almost empty water container, Brun straightened up and began to walk. The others were just reaching the rocks, where there was shelter.

They had found a little shade. The guide had crossed to the far side, taking up a half-shaded position from which he could watch. The wounded man also had found a good fighting position.

Sweat dripped down Brun's face. He was surprised there was so much moisture left in his parched body, for his lips were cracked, and his eyes smarted from sunburned rims. He tried putting a small round rock in his mouth, but it produced little saliva.

One by one he studied the men as they rested. That they had come so far was a miracle, but they must still move on.

If there was water near Mount Ararat's foothills, as the guide believed, they would wait there, refresh themselves, and then set out again.

Brun knew what he hoped the Cimmerians did not know: that there was no relief. There were no other warriors to come looking for them; and in all that vast wasteland of the Assyrian highland there was no one from whom they could expect help.

At the Fort, on the west side of Lake Van near Tuspha, they had ridden out expecting to gain some knowledge of the country, but so far they had lost a leader and four warriors.

The one thing that the Cimmerians had that Brun and the patrol's survivors didn't have, was plenty of water.

Brun considered the odds and found no comfort in them. His men lacked water and were obviously dehydrated, some in much worse shape than others. He knew the signs. None of the men complained; they were beyond that. From their flushed skin, labored breathing, and sleepiness, he could judge their degree of exhaustion.

If they could get water tomorrow, all would be ok. At sundown, Brun got them up. They moved out, scattered a little, making a poor target in the dim light, and again the Cimmerians did not launch any arrows.

Brun looked at the mountain peak of the foothills before them, and headed for it. As mountains went, it wasn't much, but it was their landmark, it was their hope.

They were far to the northwest of Lake Van now. As they moved ahead, the Cimmerians came closer. Deliberately Brun stopped, dropped to one knee on the blistering sand and held his bow and sighed his arrow on the nearest Cimmerian. He faced the situation calmly. The Cimmerian stopped.

Brun had been close to death too many times not to know that he was living on borrowed time. If there was water there they would drink, and if there was no water they would die.

As they got to the water hole and found it dry, Brun put down his bow, unslung the arrows, and went into the basin. Throwing aside the slabs of cracked earth, he began to dig. The earth at the bottom was sand and clay, and it was very dry like something that had been in the sun for years.

On his knees, Brun worked with his hands, digging, he didn't think about the parched earth. He didn't think about the sting of the soil when it got into cuts on his hands; he thought only of the water below. Brun went on digging. The work was harder, for the sand was firmly packed, but he gouged out great handfuls and tossed them on the growing bank. At last, he saw moisture at the bottom of the hole. He sat back, hands hanging, and watched. Slowly, water began to seep into the hole.

He dipped up a little, and touched his lips with it, letting a few drops fall on his tongue. A drop or two went down his throat, and he felt a delicious coolness go all through him. When he could get a few mouthfuls down his throat, he took up his bow and walked out to where the others sat.

"Thank Abzu"[2] he said "We have water."

Shortly before midnight on the twenty-first day after the four men had left the Fort, they returned. The Fort had miserable shelters, but there was water there, there was food, and there was rest.

"Brun?" The voice of a warrior at the Fort spoke and was brisk.

"Our Scythian King Bartatua would like to see you at once."

---

[2] Note: Abzu is the god of fresh water.

Their Migration Experiences

Chapter Six: The Caucasus, Thrace, and the Black Sea

Inscriptions are often cited as a link between the deported Israelites, the Cimmerians and the Scythians (Saka).

The Cimmerians or Gimirri, who first appeared in Assyria and Media in the seventh century BC have names identical with the Israelite Beth-Khumree (house of Omri) of Samaria. The Behistun Rock that was inscribed by King Darius of Persia, nearly two centuries later confirms that their names are identical.

The terms *Cimmerian* and *Scythian* were interchangeable. *Gimirrai (Gamir)* was the normal designation for *Cimmerians* as well as *Scythians* in Akkadian." The Greeks called the Scythians, Iskuza *Skuthaen or Skuthai*. The Behistun inscriptions were written in three languages much like the Rosetta Stone of Egypt. They were in Persian, Susian (Elamite or Median), and Babylonian (Akkadian) with each arranged parallel one to another.

The Behistun Rock describes Skuka, king of the subjugated Asiatic branch of Scythians, pictured as the last one in a line. In both the Persian and Elamite versions the original word is *Sakka (Saka or Sakai)*, but in the Babylonian version the same people are called *Gimiri*.

As a side note, there are similarities between the King of Northern Israel Jehu's pointed headdress in the Black Obelisk inscriptions from an earlier time and that of the captive Saka king that is portrayed on the Behistun Rock.

The Rock Inscriptions list 23 provinces, which constituted the Persian Empire in about 520 BC. The 19th province listed, in the *Persian* language, is called *Scythia*; phonetically it is *Saka*. It is *also* named *Scythia* or *Sakka* phonetically in the *Susian* or

Median language. However, in the *Babylonian* language, that same province is called *the land of the Cimmerians* and phonetically *Gimir*.

The Gimira are identified as being exiles from another land and were in areas where the Assyrians had placed some Israelites tribes.

According to Assyrian documents, the Cimmerians are continuously in the midst of battle between the armies of Urartu and Assyrian in towns to the east into Media and to the west between Lake Van and Lake Urmia.

Cimmerians and Herodotus

In about 674 to 673 BC, the Medes, Cimmerians, and Mannaeans, who were led by Phraortes' son, rebelled against their overlord, King Esarhaddon of Assyria. In the revolt, which took place near Parsua, west of Media and north of Ellipi and Elam, the Assyrians were open to attack

by the Cimmerians, who were now allies of the Medes.

Subria, the country west of Lake Van, was also invaded by the Cimmerians in about 672 or 669 BC.

Herodotus writes regarding the King of Lydia, Ardys II who lived from 678 to 629 BC who wrote about the pursuit of Cimmerians by the Scythians. Ardys' states that the Cimmerians were driven from their homes by the nomads of Scythia. They entered Asia and in his reign captured Sardis, all but the citadel. Ardys II reigned forty-nine years, and was succeeded by his son, Sadyattes, son of Ardys II who was also King of Lydia from 624 to 619 BC.

Herodotus wrote of a second battle between the Cimmerians and Scythians: He said the Median King Cyaxares, who reigned from 624 to 585 BC, had begun a siege of Nineveh, which led to the defeat of the Assyrians, when a numerous horde of Scythians, entered Median territory under their king Madyes, son of Bartatua. They were the same Scythians who had burst into the region in pursuit of the Cimmerians, whom they had driven out of Europe earlier .

The Scythians

Around 676 BC, the Scythians led by Ishpaki in alliance with the Mannaeans attacked Assyria. The group first appears in Assyrian annals under the name Ishkuzai. According to Esarhaddon's inscription, the Assyrian empire defeated the alliance. Subsequent mention of Scythians in Babylonian and Assyrian texts occurs in connection with Media.

As noted, after the Phraortes' death in 653, the Medes came under rule of the Scythians who had invaded Urartu, a kingdom already seriously weakened by its long struggle against Assyria.

Evidence of the Scythian's presence comes from an archaeological dig. In Ziwiye, on the south of Lake Urmia, a Scythian castle was unearthed from about 650 BC and the most important find was a bronze sarcophagus or coffin among other gold personal ornaments. On the rim of the coffin's lid was inscribed a scenes of Median and Urartian tribute-bearers being ushered into the presence of an official of exalted rank. The person depicted on the rim was neither an Assyrian governor nor an Urartian or Median king, nor the Mannaean king, but it was Bartatua, *the Great Scythian king*, who died about 645 BC.

By Bartatua's marriage with the Assyrian royal princess, he became an Assyrian prince. The engravings suggest that under the terms of the treaty with Esarhaddon the realm of Bartatua may have been regarded by the Assyrians as a fief of Assyria, and he himself as a viceroy in charge of Media, Mannaea and Urartu. From the legal point of view, the queries imply that Bartatua, in marrying Esarhaddon's daughter, had to take an oath of allegiance and thus legally became an Assyrian vassal which helped to hold the countries Bartatua ruled. Consequently, his kingdom was an extension of the Assyrian kingdom.

The agreement seems to have worked for in about 653 BC, the Assyrians defeated Media and left the country to be ruled by the Scythians who had aided them.

One of the early feats of Bartatua's son Madyes was his victory over the Cimmerians sometime after 650 BC. A study of Scythian/Assyrian relations during the second half of the seventh century BC suggests that the might of the Scythians under both Bartatua and Madyes depended in great measure on their close cooperation with Assyria.

However, the last great king of Assyria, Ashurbanipal, died in 627 BC, and the Scythians ruled Media until 625 BC when the young and very able Median king Cyaxares ascended the throne of Media.

In 615 BC, the Babylonian kingdom began attacking Assyrian cities with the help of the Medes and Assur was sacked. In the summer of 614 BC, Cyaxares marched upon Nineveh and put it under siege. Later, there was a pause in the siege when the Medes were engaged with Scythians, but the Scythians were persuaded to join the Median/Babylonian alliance.

The Gimirrai or Cimmerians never appear in conjunction with the Scythians, but always together with other northerners, the Mannai and Medians, as if allied, or at least making war in common, with them.

The final collapse of the Assyrian Empire took place

somewhere about 609 to 605 BC and then that of Urartu in the sixth century, between 590 and 585 BC.

The Israelites

In the Bible, God explains to Ezra the meaning of a dream Ezra had about a man on a mountain destroying hoards advancing to wage war against him. "Then you saw him collecting a different company, a peaceful one. They are the ten tribes which were taken off into exile in the time of King Hosea, whom Shalmaneser V King of Assyria, took prisoner [he was Tiglath Pilsner III's son who was succeeded by Sargon II]. He deported them beyond the River, and they were taken into a strange country. But then they resolved to leave the country populated by the Gentiles and go to a distant land never yet inhabited by man, and there be obedient to their laws which in their own country had failed to keep. As they passed through the narrow passages of the Euphrates, the Most High performed miracles for them, stopping up the channels of the river until they crossed over. Their journey through that region Arzareth was long, and took over a year and a half. They have lived there ever since, until this final age. Now they are on the way back."

The region they departed from to begin their trek according to Kings II would have been Harbor, Gozan, Hala, and the cities of Medes.

And according to Tobit, it would have included Nineveh and Rages in today's Iraq and Iran.

From all indications, however, people from the ten tribes assimilated early on.

Bruni's Narrative

Brun and his family, the Scythians mentioned earlier, finally caught up with their relatives in western Anatolia. Their tribe had been living in the Phrygian region and after several generations had decided to move north across the Dardanelle Straits into the Thrace region about 590 BC.

Thrace was located in today's Bulgarian region in southeastern Europe just north of the Sea of Marmara. Thracians populated the Varna area as early as 1200 BC.

Relations with the Phrygians had been good but deteriorated when the Cimmerians began to court Sargon II and the Phrygians. The Scythians decided that their best course of action was to leave. Thrace was a region where many of their relations had migrated to across the Straits, had assimilated with the locals and were now known as Celts.

The Celts were distant cousins of both the Cimmerians and Scythians, some tribes of which had migrated into Thrace and into Europe along the Danube River many millennium before.

The Chieftain of the Scythian tribe in the Phrygian region was Bruni a descendant of Brun.

Even though, many years and distance had passed since Bru, Sun and Brun lived in Saka and migrated to Anatolia via Musair, life was still difficult with day to day challenges for their descendants and others.

The following narrative is an example of life as a Scythian traveled towards the Thracian region and became part of the broader Celtic community.

The Scythian, Bruni, is on his way north to join his tribe and family in Thrace.

It was early in the day shortly after dawn when he came upon the trail of the Cimmerian war party in Phrygia. The high walls of the narrowing valley of the Sakarya River confined his route, and Bruni, knew he could have a problem.

A man of patience, he was sitting on his horse in the

shadow of trees. Behind him were his other horses carrying some of his tribes, and his family's belongings. His family and the tribe had gone on ahead to Thrace and he stayed behind to make sure that all the tribe's debts had been taken care of.

Before him the mountain slope was green with the first sign of spring. Nothing moved along that slope, nor in the valley below, only the trembling leaves of the trees. Bruni was never one to accept the appearance of things in the Phrygian's country and remained where he was.

Against the background of the trees he was invisible as long as he remained still, for his clothing, the horses, and their packs were all of a neutral color, blending well with their surroundings.

Methodically, his eyes searched the slope, sweeping from side to side, taking it all in; every clump of brush or tree, every outcropping of rock, and each change of color in the grass.

When you were in enemy country you never took a risk, whether you suspected a Phrygian fighter to be near or not. You learned also to make a fire that was small, on which to prepare your meal, and after eating to shift your camp a short distance away to sleep in darkness, without a fire.

Bruni had also learned not to show himself on the top of a ridge, nor to sleep beside a campfire. He had known men who did both and who were dead now.

These were the simple rules of survival; and besides these, there were others: never move without weapons, and observe the movements of birds and animals as indications of danger.

Bruni no longer even thought about the necessity of doing such things, for they had become as natural as breathing.

He saw that the Cimmerian war party included a dozen of the local Phrygians; and if they were headed for a raid on the settlements to the north, they might well plan a rendezvous with other Phrygians along the trail. They were only minutes ahead of him, and the question was, did they know he was behind them?

He studied the slope with a skeptical eye. Behind his easygoing way, Bruni's mind had been sharpened and his senses honed by years of experience ... living, mostly on the move.

Born in the dark forests of Anatolia at the foot of Mount Ararat, where his family had been among the first Scythians to settle. Bruni had moved west with his father to Lydia when only fifteen, and shortly after his father's death he had gone on his own, working to supply game to other people in the tribe.

In the years that followed he traveled from the Meander River in southern Anatolia to the Halys River in northern Anatolia and from the shores of the Mediterranean to the southern shores of the Black Sea.

In those years he left the countryside only twice, aside from a brief visit the historical site of Troy. Those two trips away from the country were to Smyrna and Sinope.

Now Bruni searched out the probable line of travel of the war party and studied it with care, but he could see no movement, nothing. But he recalled an old saying he had heard many years before: *When you see Phrygians, be careful. When you do not see them, be twice as careful.*

Bruni had great respect for the Phrygians. He knew of them as fierce fighting men, like Scythians, who lived for war and horses.

The Phrygians knew the wilderness, and how to live with it. They lived by their senses, and man could only survive in their country by being better prepared.

It was a lethargic kind of morning as the sun brightened the ridges behind him with light. The grass was still; the tree's leaves rustled in an intermittent breeze. His horse was impatient to go, an insect buzzed lazily in the bushes.

Below him and to the right was another, somewhat larger clump of trees. He gauged its height and his own position. To reach it he need be visible for no more than a minute.

A slight breeze moved behind him dancing the tree leaves and stirring the grass, and when the breeze and its movement reached him, he moved with its movement, keeping the first clump of trees behind him. He paused again when he had rounded the second clump, then started down the slope on the opposite angle to that he had been using.

A short distance ahead the narrow valley narrowed still more; then it widened out until it finally opened upon the plains. If the Phrygians knew of him and planned an ambush, that would be the place. Not in the narrows, but just before they were reached or just after leaving them.

He thought "Coming into a dangerous place a traveler's attention is directed ahead, toward a likely spot for an ambush, and he overlooks the ground he is just about to cross. Then after passing a dangerous place, there is a tendency to let down."

Bruni was in no hurry. Using infinite care and holding well to the side of the valley, he worked his way along the bottom of the valley, following the river and keeping close to the trees or under them.

When he reached the place where the Cimmerians had crossed, he drew up and allowed his horses to drink, and when they had drunk their fill he dismounted and drank himself, choosing a spot upstream from the horses. He was rising from the ground when he heard the horse hoofs.

He remained where he was, without changing position, listening and watching. How far off were they?

He soon saw and heard the whistle of arrows in the sky. Swinging onto the horse, he moved out, crossed the stream and pushed on, keeping in the shadow of the trees.

When he approached a rise in the ground where the stream dipped through a cut, he left the stream and mounted the rise until his eyes could look over the top. Before him lay a large grassy meadow. On his left, the waters of the stream pooled catching the sunlight and sparkling with ripples from the wind. Beyond the meadow the stream again crossed the valley to flow through the narrows along the opposite side.

At this point the walls of the mountain towered over a thousand feet above the meadow, sloping steeply up to the crests of the ridges. A man on foot might have climbed those walls at almost any point, but at no point could a horse scale them.

The launched arrows were stuck in the meadow's grass, and a horse was down with an arrow in its shoulder, threshing out its life in bitter, protesting kicks.

At first Bruni saw nothing else. The morning held still, as if waiting, a slight coolness remained in the air despite the bright sun on the ridges. The Phrygian's horse gave one last, despairing kick and died. The blood where the arrow penetrated on its shoulder was bright crimson in the sun.

And then a Cimmerian moved, Bruni immediately saw two others, their presence revealed by his suddenly focused attention. All were facing down the meadow, their backs toward him.

Obviously the Cimmerian and Phrygian warriors had ridden into an ambush. Bruni thought they must have been following a party of Scythians without being aware of it. Sitting high on his horse, he looked beyond the dead animal, and from the vantage point of the knoll he could see them clearly, five friendly Scythians lying in a depression. He guessed that their horses were hidden in the trees where the stream

again crossed the meadow, with a man or two on guard.

Near the body of the horse lay a dead Phrygian. If there were any wounded they had disappeared.

One Phrygian was dead and the Scythians were still out-numbered by them … two to one.

Searching the terrain before him, he picked out several other Phrygians. The others in the party must be hidden somewhere among the trees along the stream.

There was nothing he could do. To advance was to lay himself open to attack by the Cimmerians, and perhaps by the ambushing party, who might not recognize him as a brother Scythian.

All he could do was wait, a chance might come for him to make a run for it across the open meadow.

He was where the trees were scattered, but close on his left was the thicker forest along the stream, which meandered back and forth across the narrow valley.

Shadows fell about him and he was in a good position to remain unseen. He stayed on the horse, ready to fight or run, as the situation might demand.

Here and there mountain peaks allowed sunlight to reach the meadow and the river. Birds were singing in the bushes, and Bruni relied on them for a warning if any Phrygians started to move in his direction.

His eyes continued to search the meadow. And then he saw what he had half suspected. Two Cimmerians were creeping through the grass towards his Scythians. When the others fled, these two must have deliberately fallen from their horses in simulated death, for the sole purpose of this attack.

Lifting his bow, Bruni estimated the distance. The target was poor, the range too great. He was hesitating whether to launch a warning arrow when someone launched an arrow from the trees where he believed the Scythian's horses were hidden.

One of the Cimmerians screamed and leaped to his feet: His screams bellowed; he fell back to the grass where he struggled an instant; then relaxed and lay still.

The other Cimmerian did not move, and three searching arrows sent into the grass near him drew no response from him.

Bruni chewed on a stem of grass and thought of how combat was not as you expected it to be. Moments of smashing, thundering struggle were few; so often it was like this, a few arrows in the still air, and then endless minutes of waiting, when nothing happened.

Night vapor glistened on

the grass, and the birds were still singing. His horse stamped a restless hoof against the turf and flicked his tail. The horses cropped indifferently at the grass, or stood three-legged, heads down, dozing in the morning warmth.

The position of the Scythians was well chosen. Such an ambush in the open was a trick, and obviously the Cimmerians had been surprised by the use of their own tactics.

Counterattack on the part of the Phrygians was difficult, because of the Scythians in the trees near the stream.

Yet if the stalemate continued until dark, the excellent position of the Scythians would be worthless, for the superior numbers of the Phrygians could close in quickly.

The Scythians had laid their ambush, but now they faced danger. When they failed to destroy the larger part of the party, they left themselves in a bad way.

For some time Bruni had realized that his own position was increasingly perilous. Other Phrygians might come to rendezvous with these, or some Cimmerian might move back far enough to discover him. Once seen, cut off as he was from the other men, he would be surrounded and killed.

But a sudden attack by him now, from an unexpected quarter, might work in his favor. At that moment, when the Cimmerians were likely to be confused and uncertain, Bruni made a decision to act.

Three Phrygians were exposed to his arrows. One was some distance away, two were relatively close by. Lifting his bow, he drew and settled his aim on the spine of the nearest Phrygian. He took a deep breath, let it out easily, and released the bow string.

The arrow flew in the narrow valley, and the Phrygian at whom he put the arrow into stiffened sharply, then rolled over, face to the sky. Instantly Bruni reloaded arrows again and again.

The first arrow made was a clean hit, the second missed, and the third hit. Bruni slapped his heels into the ribs of his horse and fled across the meadow, screaming and yelling.

He counted on the sudden attack, which he had tried to make appear as coming from several men, to surprise the Cimmerians into giving him a running start.

Astonished by the attack, the Cimmerians fled for the brush, and as Bruni dashed by the depression, he saw the Scythians on their feet, launching arrows at the retreating Phrygians. Drawing up among the trees, Bruni saw a lean, powerful Scythian drop from a tree. His name was Wil.

"Well Bruni," the man said as he came toward him with a broad grin, "you showed up at the right time. Where did you come from?" Bruni said, "Over on the south side."

Bruni traveled with the Scythians for two days. He thought: If the Phrygians were like other friendly tribes, it would have been different. A man could get to know them and to know them was to like them. But the Cimmerian were in Anatolia courting them and no tribe was more trouble to the Scythian.

The Scythians had been able to work with the Assyrians, Kurds, Medes and others but not the Cimmerians.

Bruni rode with care until he was out of Anatolia, out of Phrygian country, and across the Straits into Thrace where he heard the Thracian King make the boast that no warrior of their tribes had ever killed a Scythian.

Bruni was ready to believe it, since getting to know someone allowed dialogue and provided an ability to settle differences!

Their Migration Experiences

Chapter Seven: The Celts

Thrace

The period of turmoil following collapse of the Mycenaean civilization in the Peloponnesian Peninsula caused whole communities to migrate from Europe into Asia Minor, trekking across the Hellespont or sailing the Aegean.

As noted earlier, Thrace was located in today's Bulgarian region in southeastern Europe just north of the Sea of Marmara. Thracians populated the Varna area as early as 1200 BC.

One of the migrating groups was the Phrygians who are thought to have come from Thrace. They established a kingdom that became the dominant Anatolian power in the 9th and 8th centuries BC.

Records exist of numerous kings, bearing alternately the names of Gordius and Midas. Their king Midas was credited by the Greeks with the power to change anything he touched into gold.

As mentioned earlier, the Scythians invaded the Cimmerians and caused two groups of them move in separate directions: one towards the southwest where they joined with the Treres of Thrace; and another body moved ahead of the Scythians towards the southeast and across the Caucasus Mountains where they threatened the Assyrians, who over time called them Gimiraa and Gameraa.

According to DNA evidence, the Scythians ended up mostly in the Slavic countries and Russia, while the Cimmerians ended up mostly in the Celtic areas of Europe including the Iberian Peninsula, Ireland, Scandinavia, and Great Britain.

Tacitus, the author of "Germaina" published in 98 AD, writes that the Cimbri (Cimmerians) were famous for their Migrations. He also states that they were known as early as 113 BC for their migration into Gaul.

The earliest Greek archaeological material is dated from about 600 to 575 BC or, according to Pseudo-Scymnus, it was in the time of Astyages the last king of the Median Empire. Pseudo-Scymnus is a name given by Augustus Meineke to an unknown author of geography written in Greek on the Circumnavigation of the Earth. It is a summary of information on the coasts of Spain, the Black Sea and data on various Greek and Thracian colonies.

There were many tribes of barbarians in antiquity and they were most often referred to in a polemic manner. They are mentioned in the "Chonicon Paschale," a Byzantine 7th-century universal chronicle of the world. Its unknown Greek author named it *Epitome of the ages from Adam the first man to the 20th year of the reign of Heraclius* who was a Byzantine Emperor from 610 to 641 AD.

The Chonicon reads, "The parents of all the heresies, and the prototypes from which they derive their names, and from which all other heresies originate, are these four primary ones. The first is Barbarism, which prevailed without a rival from the days of Adam through ten generations to the time of Noah. It is called Barbarism, because men had no rulers, nor submitted to any particular discipline of life; but as each thought proper to prescribe to himself; so he was at liberty to follow the dictates of his own inclination. The second is Scythism which prevailed from the days of Noah and thence downwards to the building of the tower and Babylon, and for a few years subsequently to that time, that is to the days of Phaleg and Ragau [Phaleg is also called Peleg and his father is called Heber. Phaleg's son is called Ragau or Reu]".

The Chonicon continues "But the nations which incline upon the borders of Europe continued addicted to the Scythic heresy, and the customs of the Scythians to the age of Thera [Santorini eruption], and afterwards; of this sect also were the Thracians."

Thracian sites have shown uninterrupted occupation from the 7th to the 4th century BC. Artifacts from these sites indicate that they had close commercial relations with others in the trading colony.

The Greek alphabet has been applied to inscriptions in Thracia since at least the 5th century BC; and the Hellenistic city worshipped a Thracian great god.

Herodotus refers to the Thracian tribe of Getae as having one God and believing in immortality and resurrection.

Their God was Zalmoxis, a man from Samos and, a slave of Pythagoras the son of Mnesarchus.

Zalmoxis, originally from Thrace, left Samos returning to Thrace and taught his former country men, the Greek way of life. Zalmoxis was a legendary social and religious reformer, regarded as the only true god by the Thracian Dacians who were also known in the Greek records as Getae.

Josephus wrote that Tiras was ancestor of the Thirasians (Thracians). These were the first fair-haired people mentioned in antiquity according to Xenophanes, and were later known as the Getae (and later Goths) according to historians beginning with Herodotus. Xenophanes was a Greek philosopher, poet, and social and religious critic.

Some scholars have suggested that Tiras was worshiped by his descendants as Thor, the god of thunder, equating both these forms with the Thouros mentioned by

Homer as the Mars of the Thracians.

In referring to how people view their Gods, Xenophanes states that the Thracians say that Gods have blue eyes and red or blond hair." He states "In the North The roving Scythian, with his carrot curls and flaring cattish eyes, must lend his mould to heaven's high lord; and so we make our gods in our own likeness, and we cringe the knee before the magnified deformity of our poor human selves."

According to Herodotus, another Scythian tribe, north of the Black Sea, the Budini, were people with bright red hair and deep blue eyes.

Tiras or Tyras in antiquity was also the name of the Dniester River and of a Greek colony situated near its mouth.

The earliest Norse sagas name Thor as an ancestral chieftain, and trace his origins to Thrace.

The Danube River

Trade usually followed migration paths. Ancient geographers often wrote about the migration routes of nomads that extended from the greater part of southeastern Europe and Central Asia. Their travels extended eastward from the Carpathian Mountains to the Don River and southeast from the Danube River to the mountains of Turkistan.

Sometime around 6200 BC, nomads began to settle along the Ister River, which is today's Danube bringing with them agricultural technology, grains, livestock and flint tools. Around 5000 BC, copper smelting was discovered as well as the development of means to replace stone tools and implements with that of copper.

This was the beginning of the Copper Age and established the Danube region as a gateway for trade with other regions in today's Europe, the Near East, and Mediterranean. By about

4000 BC, agricultural settlements in Greece, Turkey, Hungary, and the Balkans became substantial with good houses, pottery, metal tools, and implements, as well as trade networks linking the settlements together.

The Danube River is navigable for much of its route and has always played an important role in the commerce of Europe. It is the second longest river in Europe and flows about 1770 miles from its western source in the Black Forest region of Germany, about 20 miles from the Rhine, near Lake Constance to its mouth at the Black Sea on today's Romanian coast. Today the Danube is a popular destination, coupled with adjacent waterways, for river cruises.

Aristotle says the source of the Danube is in the land of the Celts; that it rises near the Celtic city of Pyrene; and that the Celts lived west of the *Pillars of Hercules* (the Straits of Gibraltar) next to the *Cynetoi*, who were the westernmost peoples of Europe. Today this is the southeast region of Portugal known as the Algarve's Region.

Celts and Descendants

Herodotus states that the tribes who live north of the Ister (Danube) are called Sigynnae and dress like Medians. Their horses have shaggy hair all over their bodies, as much as five fingers long. They are small and too weak to carry men. However, when yoked in chariots and driven by natives they are very high-spirited.

The Sigynnae boundaries extend to the parts near the Enetoi, who live on the Adriatic. The Enetoi, today's Veneti, were an ancient people who inhabited northeastern Italy.

A Celtic Veneti tribe was also a maritime power in southwest Brittany.

According to Caesar, the Celtae were an ancient people of Thrace from near the mountains of Rhodope and Haemus. They were later located in Gaul, in that part called Gallia Comata between the Garonne and Seine, from whom that country was likewise called Gallia Celtica. They were the most powerful of the three great nations that inhabited Gaul, and are supposed to be the original inhabitants of that extensive country. It is generally supposed that they called themselves Gail, or Gael, out of which name the Greeks formed their name Keltai, and the Romans called them Galli. Some however, deduce the name from the Gaelic Ceilt, an inhabitant of the forest.

Aristotle reports on them as neither dreading earthquakes, nor inundations, rushing armed into waves and plunging their newborn infants in cold water, or clothing them in scanty garments.

In other works attributed to him, he speaks of the British island as lying above the Celts.

Aristotle speaks of Keltica, and the Iberians and places the Celts above Iberia. He almost speaks of global warming by stating, ". . . we should rather say, that the temperature of France has been softened, by the demolition of its forests, the disappearance of its marshes, and the cultivation of its soil."

Poseidonius was a major source of information on the Celts of Gaul and was quoted by Timagenes (a Greek who wrote about the Celts around 56 BC), as well as Julius Caesar, the Sicilian Greek Diodorus Siculus, and the Greek geographer Strabo.

Tacitus, the Roman historian who lived from 56 to 117 AD, wrote "Germania" which describes the lands, laws, and customs of the tribes. History records the migration to Europe of Celtic tribes, some into Jutland and others into

Gaul. In the Levant, the Hellenistic and Roman conquerors from about 300 BC to 200 AD renamed the area of Gilead (Golan) which was the previous home of the exiled Israelite tribes of Gad, Reuben and half of Manasseh. In Hebrew, it is Golan and in Greek, it is Gaulanítis.

In another reference to the Celts being in the extreme west, Herodotus states ". . . the Celts, who, save only the Cynetes, are the most westerly dwellers in Europe." The main city of the country of the Cynetes or Conii was Conistorgis, which probably means City of the Conii. According to Strabo, who considered the region Celtic; he writes "In the country of the Celti, Conistorgis is the best known city"

Near current day Lagos in the Algarve Region of Portugal in the Southwest portion there is evidence of Phoenician presence around the seventh century BC. The city was founded by the Conii (or Cynetes) around 1899 BC.

Herodotus makes reference to Celts in his Histories, though he admits that his information about the west is imperfect. He provides three geographical facts related to what Aristotle mentioned earlier, that that the source of the Danube is in the land of the Celts; that it rises near the Celtic city of Pyrene; and that the Celts lived west of the Pillars of Hercules (Straits of Gibraltar) next to the Cynetoi (Cynesii or Cynetes), who were the westernmost peoples of Europe.

Herodotus actually said, "This latter river [the Ister or Danube] has its source in the country of the Celts near the city Pyrene, and runs through the middle of Europe, dividing it into two portions. The Celts live beyond the Pillars of Hercules, and border on the Cynesians, who dwell at the extreme west of Europe. Thus the Ister flows through the whole of Europe before it finally empties itself into the Euxine at Istria, one of the colonies of the Milesians."

Archaeologists report that during the second half of the first millennium BC the area of Europe north of the Mediterranean world shared two related cultures. From the British Isles to the headwaters of the Danube to the eastern fringe of the Alps existed what historians label the Hallstatt Celtic culture and later the La Tène Celtic culture.

The center of the La Tène region, which began to flourish during Herodotus' time, was close to the source of the Danube and eventually covered most of Western Europe, where the Celts lived. The center of the La Tène region could very well be a proper location for that ancient city of Pyrene.

There is a village in the La Tene region of Southern Germany called Heuneburg. It is near the head of the Danube and excavations indicate it may be the ancient city of Pyrene.

The Halstatt Culture

The Halstatt Civilization in its strict sense began well after 700 BC with the arrival of tribes from the east. The *Britannica* states that it is generally agreed that the Celts came from the east by the valley of the Danube.

The Urnfield Culture was dominant in Central and Western Europe in about 1200 BC out of which developed the Halstatt Culture which was followed by the La Tène Culture and covered much of Western Europe.

The transition from Urnfield to Halstatt cultures was around 700 BC and was caused by groups of conquerors from the east identified as Cimmerians. The cultures occupied the later general area of the Great Moravia region above the Danube River.

Moravia is a historical region in Central Europe in the east of the Czech Republic, together with Bohemia and Silesia one of the former Czech lands. It takes its name from the Morava River that is north of the Danube and which rises in the northwest of the region and flows south past the capital of the region and ancient city of Brno.

About 700s BC there appeared in Hungary, and southwestward, bronze horse bits and bridle mounts that are closely related in form to types found across the Pontic steppe in Caucasia and even farther afield in Persia.

The Celtic Hallstatt culture and the Scythian Vekerzug or Thracian culture are examples of how closely the peoples interacted with one another. Vekerzug is a burial ground of the Scythian period, dating from the sixth to fourth centuries BC, located near the city of Szentes in the Tisza river basin in Hungary. More than 150 burials in shallow pits were excavated. Some were cremations with ashes in urns and among them were clay vessels, bronze ornaments, paste beads, iron knives, spearheads, swords, and bronze Scythian arrowheads. Burials of horses were also discovered and some with remains of chariots. The finds indicate that the local population maintained relations with the Scythians and Thracians.

During the Late Hallstatt period from the mid-sixth to mid-fifth centuries BC, most of the central and eastern Carpathian basin was populated with people known from the Vekerzug site.

Those who established the Hallstatt Culture from about 700 to 450 BC were Celts who were innovative metalworkers.

Many of the richest Hallstatt burial places contained four-wheeled wagons. Their spoke wheels were fitted with iron tires shrunken and nailed around the composite wooden rims. Their wooden yokes were decorated by patterns of bronze nail heads.

The Hallstatt Culture spread with the Celts through much of western Europe between the 7th and 4th centuries BC. Their sites seem to have been concentrated initially from the area of the Upper Danube to Bohemia that today is located in the Czech Republic in the Prague region. Later in the 500s BC, however, their zone of control expanded to the west.

The Celts were also identified with the La Tène Culture from about 450 to 458 BC, which owed much of its development to the Hallstatt.

The Halstatt civilization of central and Western Europe was taken over by a group that exhibited wagon burials, long Assyrian type swords, and a peculiar type of helmet. The type of helmet had been used by horsemen in Israel and by horsemen in Assyrian service, which afterwards was thought to be typically Scythian.

In the early Halstatt culture, the newcomers introduced an increased social hierarchy, more warlike characteristics of the richer graves, greater use of the horse by the upper classes, and burial by inhumation rather than cremation that the previous Urnfield culture had practiced.

In this period, some signs of Assyrian domination or presence were also evident in Britain, Spain, and Scandinavia. If the bearers of this influence were not Assyrians then at least they were peoples who had been strongly influenced by Assyrians in the recent past.

European military helmets following the Hallstatt era were of Assyrian type. The earliest examples of these helmets may be those found in Denmark from about 700 BC or earlier. Vessels exhibited handle attachments similar to the Assyrian prototypes with moveable rings that characterize the cauldron founds in Copenhagen, Denmark and in Italian Cumae, a town founded by Greek Aeolians near Naples in Italy. Cumae was also the location of a people named Cimmerii.

As mentioned above, at the time the center of Halstatt Civilization was being conquered, a different group gained control of Hungary to the east. This second entity had emerged from Anatolia after 660 BC and smashed the Illyrian power in the Balkans. They are identifiable as another group of Cimmerians or Scythians. Their horse gear connects them to the Caucasus and Median areas, and reveals them to have been close culturally to the Scythians. This second element practiced burial of their chieftains in wagons as evidenced by remains which have been excavated.

There are signs in Europe of Assyrian influence which indicates that Cimmerians had Israelites with them as they came north and westward around 650 BC.

The 14th century Austrian Chronicle purports to trace an early Jewish settlement in Germany or Austria. The Chronicle connects the Dukes of Austria with Jews rather than Assyrians and states that Central Europe came to accept Jewish customs and ideas from 708 to 704 BC.

It is interesting to note how Asia Minor, Syria, and the far-off kingdom of Urartu around Lake Van contributed to the metal embossing of prehistoric Europe and the Halstatt period after 600 BC.

Both the Greeks and Phoenicians influenced this type of art and in a broad sense, the term Phoenician includes Israelite. The Neo-Assyrian era is associated with the emergence of Israelite exiles.

The Cimmerians north of the Black Sea were responsible for the appearance of a group of novel metal types associated with the bridle bits and harness of horses.

Cimmerian migrations may be traced from the Assyrian-dominated Middle East across Europe into Britain. The Cimmerians were noted for their equestrian abilities, as were the exiled Israelites with whom they were likely associated.

Tombs and Art

The Hallstatt Celts' lifestyle had many similarities to that of the Scythians. A Hallstatt sword in Vienna's Natur-Historisches Museum has ornamentation that shows a Celt wearing profusely decorated trousers. This is comparable to the Scythian dress as pictured on the gold vase from Kelerms kurgan near the Black Sea.

A Celtic sword found at Port Bern, Switzerland, was stamped during its manufacture with a decoration of two standing horned animals flanking a tree of life, which is a classic Near Eastern, Scythian theme. It is similar to the typical Scythian Akinakes sword.

History

The Britannica states that Celt is the generic name of an ancient people, the bulk of whom inhabited the central and western parts of Europe.

When the ancient Celts are mentioned by the Greek and Roman writers, they are placed in France, and Spain, and emerging into Italy.

When Greek history begins the Keltoi and afterwards the Galatai were the same as the Galli (the Gauls), and the Keltoi were one of the branches of the Cimmerian stock. Caesar says that they called themselves Celtae or Keltae though the Romans gave them the designation of Galli.

Pausanias, a Greco-Roman Geographer who lived about

150 AD says that the Celts have lately called themselves Galatai. They anciently called themselves Keltoi, and so did others.

By the early Iron Age, beginning about 1000 BC, the tribes of the central European Urnfield culture were expanding along the principal river routes, giving rise to such major groupings as the Celts and the Slavs, as well as Italic-speakers and Illyrians. One of the Illyrian tribes, the Breuci, warred with the Romans and was defeated and a number of Breuci settled in Dacia. It is likely that the northeastern Bosnian city Brčko is named after this tribe.

The Celts had widely spread on the Continent and the classical writers state that the Celts were in France about 600 years before the Christian era. Their population was so abundant, that their chiefs recommended two of their princes to lead a numerous body over the Alps into Italy. One large multitude passed into Italy near Turin, defeated the Etrurians or Tuscans while another party settled about Brixia and Verona.

Milan was founded by the Celts in approximately 600 BC.

Knowledge of the Celts grew slowly before the fourth century BC. One of the earliest references, which may contain material going back to the sixth century, was preserved by the Roman poet Avienus. In his work, Ora Maritima (The Maritime Shores or Sea Coasts) which was written at the end of the fourth century AD; he quotes from authors many of whose texts no longer exist. Among them was the early sailing manual referred to earlier as the Massaliote Periplus.

This lost work is thought to date to as early as the 6th century BC and provides information about the Atlantic seaways and the tin-producing regions.

Avienus makes only one direct reference to the Celts

when he mentions that beyond the tin-producing Oestrymnides (Extreme West) a name given to present day Portugal was a land now occupied by the Celts, who took it from the Ligurians. Liguria was composed of ancient people who lived in Southwestern Europe. The existence of the name at an early date is interesting as well as his naming of Britain as Albion and of Ireland as Ierne (Old Irish Erin, modern Eire, and Roman Hibernia). Both names are widely accepted to be in an early form of Celtic.

According to Ephorus, by the fourth century BC the Celts occupied a large swath of western Europe from Iberia to the Upper Danube and were one of the four great barbarian peoples of the world, along with the Scythians, Persians, and Libyans.

In the Teutonic language, the word German is the same as the word Belgae in the Kymric language; meaning war-men or warriors.

The Belgae of the Continent were Kymry, not Kelts, and were descendants of the Kymry who conquered the country under Brennus, and in Cesar's time occupied one third of Gaul.

Homer is one of the mutative forms of the word Gomer with the "g" dropped in translation to Greek. The Epic Poem of the Iliad on the Fall of Troy, assigned to Homer, is a collection of Heroic Ballads of the Gomeridae or Kymry on the great catastrophe of their race in the East. It was originally composed in the Kymric or Poetic characters. These were afterwards changed by the Greeks into the Phoenician, and in so doing, they dropped the Cymric radical "Gw".

In 387 BC, Brennus led an army of Cisalpine Gauls in their attack on Rome. On June 6th 363 BC Brennus' army met Rome's army at the confluence of the little river Allia with the Tiber. The Romans were routed with great slaughter; and Rome itself, with the exception of the capital, fell three days afterwards into the hands of the conqueror.

Brennus was a legendary king of Northumberland and was the son of Dunvallo King of Cornwall. According to Caesar and others however, the Brennus who attacked Rome was a chieftain of the Senones, a Gallic tribe originating from the modern areas of France known as Seine-et-Marne and Loiret. A painting shown by Paul Jamin done in 1893 and titled "Brennus and His Share of the Spoils" shows the terror of captives taken following battle.

According to Dionysius, a Greek Historian, one of the great movements of the Celts, into the Italian States, occurred when the Brennus led them to attack Rome, in which they became masters of the city, killed its senate, and had nearly

taken its capital, when Camillus, 446-365 BC a Roman soldier and statesman, rescued the republic from the barbaric conquerors.

One hundred and ten years after the first Brennus, Greece suffered an invasion of the Celts under the second Brennus, they moved through Illyria, into Macedonia and Thrace, onto Thessaly, passed the ancient strait of Thermopylae (Hot Gates) and proceeded to attack Delphi. These events occurred about 279 BC.

A Greek coalition at the narrow pass of Thermopylae, on the east coast of central Greece defended an initial assault by Brennus' forces who suffered heavy losses. Brennus then decided to send a large force against Aetolia in Anatolia. The defending Aetolian detachment, as Brennus hoped, left Thermopylae to defend their homes.

The Aetolians joined the Gauls as a group and resorted to skirmishing tactics after realizing that the Gallic sword was dangerous only at close quarters.

According to Pausanias, only half the number of Gauls that had set out for Aetolia returned – some remained to form the Galatian Region in Anatolia. Eventually Brennus found a way around the pass at Thermopylae but the Greeks escaped by sea. Brennus pushed on to Delphi where he was defeated and forced to retreat, after which he died of wounds sustained in the battle.

During the reign of Alexander the Great, Byzantium was forced to recognize Macedonian control and under his successors, the Byzantines regained independence. The city was subsequently attacked by the Scythians, and in 279 BC, the Celts, having overrun neighboring Thrace, imposed tribute on the city.

Saxons

Ptolemy says that the Scythians descended from the Sakae who had come from Media and came to be known by the name of Saxons.

Albinus, a historian who lived in the first century BC, also says, "The Saxons were descended from the ancient Sacae in Asia, and in process of time they came to be called Saxons."

Ptolemy was the first writer known to have mentioned the Saxons. He writes "By the passage in his Geography, and by the concurrence of all their future history, it is ascertained, that, before the year 141 of our era, there was a people called Saxones, who inhabited a territory at the north side of the Elbe, on the neck of the Cimbric Chersoneses, and three small islands, at the mouth of this river."

The Cimbri, the Chauci, the Suevi, the Boii, the Suardones,

and the Catti, were identical with the Saxons.

Pope Pius II, in his Historia Bohemica, says, the Saczania is one of the rivers which the Multavia (Vltava in Moldavia) receives. He says that an episode related to this was, the Galli Boii who were driven over the Saczania were called Saxons.

He also says the Suardones of Tacitus are said to be the Saxons; a name distorted by negligent transcribers because Saxones might easily slip into Sardones, and that into Suardones.

The Pope also says that it is probable that some of the marauding Sakai, or Sacassani, were gradually propelled to the western coasts of Europe, on which they were found by Ptolemy, and from which they molested the Roman Empire, in the third century of our era.

There were a people called Saxoi, on the Euxine, according to the geographical lexicographer Stephanus of Byzantium.

Tacitus, who wrote of Germany many years before Ptolemy used the name Fosi, a Germanic tribe of warriors who acquired afterwards the name of Saxons.

Marcianus of Heraclea, somewhat later than Ptolemy, gives the Saxons the same position on the neck of the Cimbric Chersoneses and that Stephanus, of Byzantium, also says that the Saxones were "dwelling in. the Cimbric Chernoesus."

According to Encyclopaedia Britannica, the Angli (Angles) definitely had a close affinity with the Saxons. The Story of English states, "To this day the [cultural] gap between the English on the one hand and the Welsh, the Scots and the Irish on the other, is often huge. To the Celts, their German conquerors (Angles, Jutes and Saxons) were all Saxons".

Anglo-Saxons

The Anglo-Saxons moved from the Cymbric peninsula, and its vicinity, in the fifth and sixth centuries AD, into England. For a long time, these tribes had harassed people in the western regions of Europe and when the provinces of Rome were overrun by Gothic nations, the Anglo-Saxons invaded Britain soon after the Romans left.

The ancient inhabitants of Britain, and many of the Romans, disappeared as the new conquerors advanced and Saxon laws, Saxon language, Saxon manners, government, and institutions were imposed.

The Anglo-Saxon conquest of Britain was divided into two phases: the first, from 280 to 450 AD, when the Saxons periodically raided the coast of Britain and returned home. The second was from 450 to 600 AD, when the Roman garrisons withdrew from Britain and the Angles and Saxons, landed and settled in various parts of the country.

The English language, government, and laws, display its Gothic heritage in every part. Not only records and traditions, but both formal and informal institutions.

The Anglo-Saxons, Lowland Scotch, Normans, Danes, Norwegians, Swedes, Germans, Dutch, Belgians, Lombards, and Franks, have all sprung from the terms Scythian, German, or Gothic.

The Jutes, Angles and Saxons came from the Baltic Sea area, and their ocean-borne raids on England were heavy and continuous. Later, by invitation of the British to exercise control over enemies, they settled along the eastern shores, in East Anglia, Mercia, Northumbria, Sussex, Wessex, Essex, and Kent.

These people who overran the British Isles were in many respects the same as the Celts who were already living there.

The invasion of the Saxons, the Goths, the Danes and the Normans changed the language of Britain, but added no new physical element. The Celts and Saxons are all one.

The Anglo-Saxon Chronicle written in about 891 AD states "The first inhabitants [of England] were Britons, who came from Armenia." Some people argue that compilers of the "Anglo-Saxon Chronicle" used the word Armenia by mistake. They cite the fact that "A History of the English Church and People" by Bede, which was used as one of the sources for the "Chronicle," has a similar sentence using the word "Armorica" instead referring to the Brittany region. The "Anglo-Saxon Chronicle" was a monumental work however, overseen by many people.

Lyson also traces the Cimbri to Armenia. Bede may have known that the migration of Britain's ancestors started in Armenia and passed through Armorica before arriving in Britain.

Tacitus writes that the Cimbri, in his time, were a small remnant of what they were, but their fame was world-wide. He said that traces of their past greatness were still to be seen, stretching in the shape of vast encampments along both banks of the Rhine River, He goes on to say that, by measuring the encampments, one can verify the enormous number of men employed and the historical truth of that swarming migration.

He said it was six hundred and forty years after the founding of Rome, that the first clash of the Cimbrian arms was heard.

He states that the peninsula of Denmark is sometimes called the Cimbric Chersonese; but there is a dispute as to its having been the original seat of the Cimbri, who invaded the Roman empire in 113 BC, when their warriors are said to have been a quarter of a million.

As noted earlier, the Celts in Thrace and Europe were mostly Cimmerians and the Slavs and Russians were mostly Scythians. The Cimmerians migrated from Thrace and became known by many different name and sub-group naming. They became the Cimbri, Celts, Gauls, Teutons, and Tuetones, plus many other sub-groupings.

There were about 300,000 Cimbri (or Celts) at the battle at Aquae Sextiae which was in southern France in the Provence region. The Romans under Gaius Marius defeated the Cimbri and Teutones who were virtually wiped out. The Romans claimed to have killed 90,000 and captured 20,000, including large numbers of women and children.

The fighting strength of the Cimberi was 300,000; not the whole people including women, children, and a great many other non-combatants. The Cimbri expedition in that battle involved all most all their people. The Cimbri left at home only a small remnant of their people.

Some branches of the Celtic peoples were primarily pastoral, others agricultural, depending on both the environment and the length of time the group had occupied their land.

Celtic wealth was divided between group members who stayed on the ancestral lands, and others who received their share in animals then moved on. It was to one's advantage to work and cooperate with the tribe.

Brunin's Narrative

This story picks up with a Cimmerian named Brunin who was a distant descendant of Ra and Brea and their children who lived on the north shore of the Black Sea about 750 BC. It was their tribe that was invaded by the Scythians who chased some of the Cimmerians south into the Caucasus' while other Cimmerians left and moved into Thrace and Europe. Ra's descendants in Thrace remained for hundreds of years up to the time of this episode in about 113 BC.

Brunin's Cimmerian or Cimbri family had a good wagon, and two good horses pulling it. The horse's harness was decorated with gold symbols. One might even think that the family was prosperous, considering they had in addition to the horses and wagon six big boys and three little girls. They didn't have wealth however, but they were hopeful.

They were heading north for open land that was free for the taking, if Romans didn't engage them first in battle.

While Brunin was a Celtic warrior, he had been recently selected to be a scout for the tribe, since he knew some of the Roman language and their customs.

The story begins with him scouting the Romans in the Vauchuse region:

There was no sound but the walking of the horse and the creak of the horse's leather bridle. The walls in the canyon rose high above Brunin as he rode, on-guard, for around the next bend or above the next rise, the Romans might find and kill him.

The trail between the canyon walls began to rise, and suddenly he emerged upon a plateau that seemed to be like an edge of the world.

Far away and below him stretched an expanse of the same country with trees and grass in the valleys below. He turned the horse at right angles and stopped.

The ground was now gravel and rock making tracking hard. He studied the ground carefully, then moved on. He was tracking one of the enemy's scouting parties that was a part of the larger Roman army.

The trail was difficult, and in the fading light, he slipped from the horse, bow and arrow in hand, and walked over the ground. The trail circled around, steadily dropping. Then ahead of him he saw a pool, and beside it a place where one could lay to drink as well as his horse.

He stripped the blanket from his horse and after watering and removing its richly decorated bridle, tethered it on a grassy plot. Then he gathered dry sticks for a fire, which he made, keeping it very small, in the shadow of some boulders.

When the fire was going, he made some broth, then slipped back from the fire and carefully scouted the surrounding area.

Every step of the way was a danger. The Romans were on the hunt now, but Brunin could fight like a cornered lion, where and when it was necessary.

Before daylight Brunin, woke, got up, packed his gear

and got the horse ready. When it was light enough to see, he saw that the trail had ended.

The water of the stream offered a path just as it had in ancient days when due to lack of trails, migration paths usually followed waterways.

The stream looked like a route the Romans would take so, he rode into it himself, scanning the banks with care.

He was slowed by his careful search for tracks, but found where the Romans had left the stream. A short distance further, after seeing no marks, he found an impression in the grass where a warrior had slipped.

He had gone no more than about an hour when he found where they had camped. There was evidence of twelve sleeping spots, with one of them back in a corner of rocks away from the other. It looked like the Roman leader was taking no chances.

As Brunin looked around, he noticed something to the

side. On the ground, it looked like the dirt had been used for planning. Scratched in the surface of the dirt, apparently with a stick, were the barely legible words "Large Green Field".

It looked like the Roman army was headed for the Large Green Field in Aquae Sextiae.

He had been thinking earlier that it was a good place for a battle.

If that was the case, it was several day's ride from where he was. Brunin thought it over while riding up the next ridge. From the out cropping, he examined the terrain before him, then had a sudden premonition.

He quickly wheeled his horse as an arrow went through his sleeve. Leaping from the horse to a hollow under an overhanging rock, he waited with an arrow ready in his bow.

The country on the other side of the ridge was fairly open, and led to the Rhone River valley, to ride down there and go after the Roman archer would be suicide. Only the wheeling of the horse had saved his life at that moment.

Sliding back from the hollow, he retreated down the slope to his horse.

He swung onto its back, and keeping the ridge between him and the unseen Roman, he started riding east.

He had made his decision, and he was going for it.

If he continued as he was now, he would fall further and further behind, being cautioned by the Roman's arrow and the difficulty of following the trail.

Brunin couldn't let the Roman army reach Large Green Field ahead of him. There would be a greater time delay and he needed to advise the Cimbri and their warriors as soon as possible as to the Roman army's intention.

He had to find a trail or a short-cut … he knew where he

was however and what may be possible.

Ahead of him, a draw opened, and he ran his horse in; it then slowed the horse. Ahead of him and on the skyline, a mountain's sharp rocky outcrop pointed at the sky. That was his landmark.

The country grew rougher, with many streams that he had to cross. He cut across a plateau to skirt a towering rust-red cliff. A notch in the cliff ahead seemed to indicate a point of entry, so he guided the horse among the landscape.

At one point, the trail was so narrow that for thirty yards, he had to lift his feet up onto the horse's neck.

Then the trail opened into a spacious green valley, its sides lined with a thick growth of trees. There was water and he stopped to give the horse a brief rest and to drink.

They had been moving at a rapid clip for the distance and the heat, yet the horse looked good. He checked his weapons, the bow, arrows, and sword.

If he was to get to Large Green Field before the Romans, he must hurry. If he failed, then there was not one chance in a thousand that he would ever see his wife again.

Now, every movement, every thought, every inflection of her voice returned to him, filling him with desperation. She was his, and had always been his, not only, he understood now, in his own heart, but in hers. However, he knew what the Roman would do if they captured her.

So on he went, the mountains grew rougher. There were more and more rocks that lasted for several hours of riding at midday under the blazing sun.

On the second day, Brunin seemed to have been going for about nine hours, yet it was only because of his early start. It was past one in the afternoon, and he had been riding, with but one break, since about four in the morning.

Large Green Field was nearer, somewhere not far from the mountain's rocky out-crop he had seen.

Sweat streamed down his face and down his body. The heat was hard to bear, since Celts loved the cold weather and were usually scantily clad.

He squinted his eyes against the sun and the smart of the sweat. He had to skirt another obstacle to get to the vicinity of Large Green Field.

He was riding now with all thought lost, only his goal in mind, and a burning, driving lust to come face to face with some Roman.

The sun brought a kind of delirium, and he thought of his wife again: He began to remember when he was injured in the last battle with the Romans; the long days of riding in a wagon, of his wife's low voice and her cool hands as he wrestled with pain and fever, recovering from the wounds of a battle; he seemed to feel again the rocking roll of the wagon over the rutted trail, tramped by thousands heading for new land or battle which ever came first.

Why had he found it hard to speak? Why hadn't he been able to find words to tell his wife how much he loved her?

Words had always left him powerless; to act was easy, but somehow to shape the things he felt into words was beyond him, and women put so much emphasis on words, on the saying of things, and the way they were said.

After a long time, he swung down from the horse and walked on, knowing even the animal's strength was not without limit. Suddenly, he arrived at Large Green Field.

The smell of the grass was rich and almost unbelievable, and he heard a bird warbling, and the sudden whir of wings as a pheasant took off in sudden flight. Water sounded, and the horse quickened its pace. Brunin skirted a wide grove of trees and rode through grass scattered with purple and pink flowers and blackberries. Then he saw the water, and rode rapidly toward it.

He dropped from the horse, taking a quick look around. No human sound disturbed the calm, utter serenity of Large Green Field. He dropped to the ground and drank, and beside him, the horse drank deep.

Suddenly, the horses head came up sharply. Warned, Brunin felt his every muscle tense. Then, he forced himself to relax. The horse was looking at something, the sound of the birds was stilled. He got slowly to his feet, striving to avoid any sudden movement, knowing in every muscle and fiber of his being that he was being watched. He turned, slowly, striving for a casual, careless manner with his hand going to his sword, his Akinakes.

A Roman scout was standing a short distance away, holding his loaded and cocked bow. He was thin but big, his face darkened by sun and wind, his eyes hard and cruel. Fear touched Brunin who said calmly. "Hello! I see you're ready to fight, Roman. You have that bow and arrow aimed where it'll do the most damage and with the arrow aimed strait at me. I see that you also have your sword it its scabbard."

The Roman smiled looking crueler than ever. "We both know what it means to have an advantage," The Roman said. "We both know it means you're a dead man." "I'm not so sure," Brunin said, shrugging. "I've heard of men who came out ahead. Maybe I'm one of the lucky ones."

What Brunin didn't know, was that his wife and children had followed the Celt warriors in the wagon along with thousands of other Cimbri families, yelling and screaming urging the warriors on into battle with the Romans.

They tended their wounded and dispatched injured enemies. They often had occasion to engage the enemy directly and it was on one occasion that Brunin's wife was captured.

The Roman laughed. "I've got the edge on two counts Cimbri. I've got a Celt woman and I think she's yours. I plan to keep her and use her! I'm pretty sure she's yours, since her husband is also a scout for the Celts. She's a redhead too, as you know. I can see in your face that she's yours, and she looks to be a hellcat too. It will be fun breaking her. I've got her, and you'll never get her back."

The Roman was wrong, he took Brunin as a prisoner and being a scout, he was held for interrogation. Several days later, as the Roman army and Celt warriors were engaged in battle at Large Green Field in Aquae Sextiae, Brunin escaped.

The Romans beat the Celts (Cimbri) in the battle at Large Green Field, but Brunin found his wife during the height of the fighting.

He was able to tell her how much he really did love her; then like all good Celts and knowing the battle was lost, he killed his wife so she couldn't suffer rape and humiliation.

He then lifted his own sword to where it was vertical to his body alongside his head with the point on his skin; he drove it down past his collar bone, into his rib cage and heart, killing himself instantly.

His children got away and lived to use their experience from this conflict to fight Romans and other tribes again in the future.

They came to be known as the Brunin Celts who lived in today's Holstein Schleswig region of Germany. They were part of the larger Angle tribe and were known as Anglos.

Brunin's descendants may have been part of the repeated Anglo-Saxon raiding parties to England that took place during Rome's last years of occupation.

Later descendants from Brunin's tribe, the De Bruni, left the Cymbric peninsula, and its lowlands, to cross the Ocean and into Britain with the Saxon leaders Hengst and Horst about 450 AD.

Their Migration Experiences

Chapter Eight: Oceans to the West, North and South

The concept of the "ocean surrounding the earth" was a prevalent idea among many early geographers. On early maps the divisions and boundaries of Europe, Asia and Africa; the Black and Caspian Seas appear close to the Northern Ocean; similar to the Persian and Arabian (Red Sea) gulfs location on the south with respect to the "circular ocean."

Marseille

The Greek colony of Massalia (Marseille), founded about 600 BC, lay in the land of the Ligurians, which was near the territory of the Celts. Also, the settlement at Narbonne was Celtic.

One example of Celts who traveled on the Ocean was the Veneti tribe as mentioned earlier. The Veneti had become a maritime power with more than 220 large oak vessels whose base of operations was in the western French peninsula of Brittany on Quiberon Bay.

Another example was the Grecian settlement of the Phocians, at Marseilles on the Mediterranean, which flourished about 540 BC. These colonists subdued some of the Celtic regions near there, founded cities and built a splendid temple to the Ephesian Diana. They raised large fleets and pursued extensive navigations. They also became distinguished for their elegance, love of literature, and spirit of philosophy. They made their city so attractive for its intellectual resources, that some of the noblest of the Romans lived at Marseilles, in preference to Athens or Rome. They introduced such a taste for Grecian customs, that the Gauls wrote their contracts in Greek.

The Celtic invaders must have brought with them artifacts picked up from their travels.

Strabo mentions, that treasures taken from Delphi, under the second Brennus' expedition were found at Tholouse by the Romans.

Ephorus remarked, that the Keltae were fond of the Greeks, and their migrations into Spain, brought them into immediate contact with the Phoenicians and Carthaginians.

The Massaliote Periplus, thought to have been written somewhere between the 6th and 3rd century BC, describes sea routes used by traders from Phoenicia and Tartessus (a harbor city in south Iberia) in their journeys around Iron Age Europe. It contained an account of a sea voyage from Massilia (Marseilles) along the western Mediterranean. It describes seaways running northwards from Cadiz in Iberia (Spain) along the coast of Atlantic Europe to Brittany, Ireland and Britain.

The Periplus is the earliest work to describe the trade links between northern and southern Europe and that such a manual existed indicates the importance of these trade links.

The trade in tin and other raw materials from the British Isles southwards is attested by archaeological evidence from this period, and earlier as well, since the riches to be won probably attracted numerous adventurers to explore and exploit the Atlantic coasts.

Pytheas, the Greek geographer and explorer from the Greek colony of Massilia (Marseille), described a similar voyage and expedition to northwestern Europe in detail, around 325 BC.

Pytheas is the first person on record to describe the Midnight Sun, polar ice, Germanic and possibly Finnic tribes. He is the one who introduced the idea of distant Thule to the geographic imagination. His account of the tides is the earliest to state they that they are caused by the moon.

The Pillars of Hercules

The Cimmerii of Homer were located by him in a land "covered in mist and cloud, nor does the sun, shining, look down on them with his rays, either when he mounts to the starry heaven, nor when he turns again to earth from heaven, but doleful night is spread over wretched folk".

To get there Ulysses, who had been sent by the enchantress Circe to consult the dead in Hades, set out from the Isle of Circe, which was itself a long way west of Greece, in the Mediterranean Sea. To reach Hades they sailed to Oceanus.

On ancient maps, Oceanus was the encircling sea that ran round all known lands and seas beyond the Pillars of Hercules (Straits of Gibraltar) and outside the Mediterranean Sea.

The realm of Hades in the Odyssey, its entrance, and outer courts, are on the western side of the river Oceanus.

Homers states that it is the abode of the Cimmerians, ". . . veiled in darkness and cloud, where the sun never shines."

Northern and German Ocean

Tacitus says that in his days, the Kimbri remained in the peninsula of Jutland. They were a small state, but great in glory. Their ancient fame was known far and wide. Their power and greatness could be measured by the reported numbers of their army. Their fame continued, in the days of Claudian, a Roman poet who lived about 365 to 404 AD who called the Northern Ocean (German Ocean or North Sea) Cimbrica Thetis (sea or ocean).

Tacitus states "The Cimbric ocean receives Rhine's flood outpoured through his two mouths."

Following the mid-5th century BC, the Cimmerians are mentioned by Strabo, as existing in his time on the Baltic, and are more briefly alluded to by Pliny. Both writers represent the Cimmerians being on the northwestern shores of Europe, or on those coasts of the German Ocean from which the Saxons and Danes made expeditions into Britain.

When the Scythians first attacked the Cimmerians on the European side of the Bosporus, the more warlike and larger part of the Cimmerians went to Asia under King Lygdamis.

Plutarch mentioned that other Cimmerians receded westward from the Scythians, and proceeded to inhabit the remoter regions of Europe, extending to the German Ocean. "Here," he adds, "it is said that they live in a dark, woody country, where the sun is seldom seen, from their many lofty and spreading trees, which reach into the interior as far as the Hercynian forest."

It was explained earlier, that the Scythians caused the Cimmerians to move westward as Celts and Gauls; that branch of Cimmerians migrated from the Black Sea region in a northwestern direction to the Low Countries that are now Belgium, Holland and Northwest Germany to the German Ocean and that they occupied the tract of land known as Cimbric Chersoneses, now called Jutland.

The Romans called these people Cimri, being an abbreviation for Cimmerians.

Plutarch in his Life of Marius says ". . . they were called at first Cimmerians and then, not inappropriately, Cimbri." He also states that Poseidonius also records the Cimbri dwelling originally on the shores of the Black Sea where they had been known to the Greeks as Cimmerians.

Historical tales of the Welsh connect themselves with the Cymry who they state were the first inhabitants of Britain and that before their arrival the region was occupied by bears, wolves, beavers, and oxen.

Their stories relate that Hu Gadarn, or Hu the Strong, or Mighty, led the nation of the Kymry through the Hazy, or German Ocean, into Britain as well as to Llydaw, or Armorica, in France; and that the Kymry (Kymri, Cymri or Cymry) originally came from the eastern parts of Europe, or near the region of present day Istanbul.

The Welsh also say that their ancestors, the Cymry, came from the regions south of the Bosporus. The Welsh add the name of their chieftain, and state that a division of the same people settled in Armorica. They talk of the memory of Lygdamis, who led the Cimmerian emigration to Asia, and of Brennus, who marched with the Celts against Greece as well as the first Brennus who marched against Rome.

These stories were preserved in the countries they overran so that the name of Hu

Gadarn was remembered on the island, which he colonized.

Armorica, or Bretagne, was peopled by a race of men similar to those who inhabited Britain, which may be verified by the close resemblance of the languages of the two countries. Tacitus says the language of the Gauls and Britons was identical.

Tacitus also says that Germany taken as a whole is divided from Gaul by the Rhine and the Danube. Mountains divide it from Sarmatia and Dacia, and on the far side it is encircled by the ocean, which sweeps around broad promontories and islands of unknown extent, where kings and tribes dwell whose existence was revealed by war.

He said that rising amid the Alps, the Rhine flows with a slight westerly curve down to its outlet in the North Sea. The Danube, issuing from the gentle slopes of the Black Forest, visits many peoples in its course until it forces its way into the Black

Sea through six mouths, while a seventh channel loses itself in the marshes.

According to most historians, the Cimmerians proceeded from the vicinity of the Cimmerian Bosporus to the German Ocean.

Their Migration Experiences

Chapter Nine: Britain

Tin was mined in Cornwall (in the southwest) from the Bronze Age. The country first became known to the Greeks about 400 BC when Pytheas of Marseille apparently visited Cornwall and a tin depot at St. Michael's Mount.

The Welsh tradition is that three groups came to Britain. The first were the nation of the Kymry, who came with Hu Gadarn to the island of Britain. He obtained not the country, nor the lands, by slaughter or contest, but with justice and peace. The other was the race of the Lloegrwys, who came from the land of Gwasgwyn; and they were of the first race of the Kymry. The third were the Brython, who came from Armorica, and who were descended from the primitive tribe of the Kymry, and they had all three the same language and speech.

This Triad offers a rough sketch of several migrations, which are seen moving towards Britain, each by a different route. The one comes over the Hazy Sea (most probably the German Ocean), and the others from Gaul across the channel. However, both are sprung of the same stock, the Kymri, the descendants of Gomer that first peopled Europe. This distinction of their origin suits the Celts who, according their tradition, were the first race of the Kymry.

The Armorican emigration was of the tribe called Brython, a name for people that Pliny called Britanni who were in Gaul in his time.

The colony from Gascony was the Lloegrwys, whose name became attached to that part of the island, which they occupied. The largest part of England has been always been referred to as Lloegr by the Welsh poets and chroniclers.

Tacitus also expressed his belief that Gauls peopled Britain and Bede derived its inhabitants as being from Armorica. What Bede didn't clarify however was whether they originally came from Armenia to Armorica.

The position of the Celts on the maritime regions of the west of Europe brought them closer to intercourse with civilized nations of antiquity who traveled on the ocean.

The latest of a series of waves of Celtic invaders comprised a group of the Gallic Belgae who overran southeastern Britain in the early part of the first century BC; and Julius Caesar felt impelled to try to round off his conquests in Gaul by invading the island in 55 and 54 BC. Thereafter its southern tribes were regarded as vassals, though they did not see themselves in this light.

Preparations for definitive conquest were made by Caligula in AD 40, but first carried out by his successor Claudius, who overran the 'Lowland Zone', captured the Belgic capital Colchester and created the new province of Britannia, a region extending from the Humber estuary to the Severn. Britannia exported grain, cattle, tin, gold, silver, iron, hides, slaves and hunting dogs for the Romans.

As mentioned, the Teutons or *Germans* migrated to England as Angles, Saxons and Jutes in the decades immediately following the departure of the Romans from Britain about 450 AD.

Prior to the migration, the Angles inhabited the area that is now known as Schleswig-Holstein, immediately south of Denmark on the Jutland Peninsula. All these tribes were Celts and many of their ancestors were Cimmerians and Scythians.

As noted earlier, the Anglo Saxons migrated to Britain under the leadership of Hengst and Horst. They moved in as the Romans left about 450 AD.

Both the Anglos and Saxons were made up of numerous tribes. The Anglos had one in particular, the De Bruni tribe. One of its leaders was a person by the name of Brunig and one of his descendants is talked about below.

Brunan's Narrative

The story begins long before Brunig's descendant, the young Anglo, met King Alfred of England. It began when the young Anglo was ten years old and first saw the Danes. It was the year 866 of the Common Era and he was his father's second son. It was the eldest who took his father's name Brunan. His brother was seventeen then, tall and well built, with his family's fair hair and his father's face.

The day the young Anglo first saw the Danes he and others were riding on a hunt along the seashore with their hawks tethered and hooded. He was riding along with his father,

his uncle brother, and a dozen men from their castle.

It was autumn and the sea cliffs were beautiful with the change in color. There were seals on the rocks, and a large number of seabirds were squawking and shrieking; too many to let the hawks off their leashes. They rode till coming to the crisscrossing shallows that rippled between the castle and a small off-shore island.

On the island, the young Anglo saw the broken walls of a building the Danes had plundered years before he was born, but the story and memory of them remained.

The young Anglo became Brunan when both his father's first son and his father was killed fighting the Danes on that day.

He gained a name but lost his lands eventually becoming a warrior and leader.

Later, the young Anglo, now Brunan, thought "My father could neither read nor write." but "Father's Priest taught me how to do both. Sometimes I take the old parchments from their wooden chest and I see the name spelled Brunan. I look at those parchments, which are deeds saying that Brunan, son of Brunan is the lawful and sole owner of the lands that are carefully marked by stones and by dykes, by oaks and by ash, by marsh and by sea."

Brunan continued to think "I dream of those lands, wave-beaten and wild beneath the wind-driven sky. I dream, and know that one day I will take back the land from those who stole it from me. The law says I own that land, and the law, we are told, is what makes us men under God instead of beasts in the field. But the law does not help me reclaim my land. The law wants compromise. The law figures that money will compensate for loss. But I am Brunan, son of Brunan and the land is mine."

Although Brunan held the paper to much land, he and his warriors were mercenaries on the move constantly repelling Danish Viking invaders or in conquering neighboring tribal kingdoms in North Umbria for others. He was often in the service of King Alfred of Wessex.

On one occasion, he and his men were outnumbered and had to flee from the invaders.

In his words he tells the story "North and westward we fled through the wind and the rain, along lonely roads, flashing through streets of settlements, our clothes ruffled in the wind, the hooves of our horses drumming stones and soil along the way. We rode through the night, through villages and on. At dawn we rested our horses in a grove beside the path we were following, and sitting under a tree, ate some of the food we brought along."

He goes on to say that as the horses grazed during a rest stop, the men talked among themselves telling of deeds and events in years gone by. Evening's vapor was upon the grass and among the dark trees. The morning sun was, lighting the mist even though the hour was early.

Brunan said to his men "I think we will be safe when we are further north in Scotland. I have not been there, but my father has, and he told me much of it. He said it was a land of barbarians and witches, where the Druids lived a time ago. We should have no trouble with any of them."

Battle of Brunanburg

Years later, when Brunan was about 80 and too old to fight battles. His son, Brunanin, lived to the west of Durham in a burg owned by the family which was named after them.

The son became engaged in one of the first large battles that would decide the fate of England. It was the "Battle of Brunanburg".

The battle was an English victory by the army of Athelstan, the King of England, and his brother Edmund (sons of King Edward and grandsons of King Alfred).

They conquered the combined armies of a Danish King; a Norse King; King Olaf of Ireland; Constantine II, King of Scots, and Owen I, King of Strathclyde.

The men who fought and died on that field made the *Battle at Brunanburh* one of the most significant battles in the long history not just of England, but of the whole of the British Isles.

The location of the battle was in the Bryneich region. It was an Anglo-Saxon region that was established by Anglo settlers of the 6th century of the Common Era in what is now southeastern Scotland and North East England.

There was in that ancient region; about five miles southwest of Durham; on the plain between the river Tyne and the river Browney, a place called Bruningafeld.

This is where the *Battle Brunanburh* was fought in AD 937.

The Anglo-Saxon Chronicles tells the story: In a preamble to an Old English Poem it states "This year [937 AD] King Athelstan and Edmund his brother led a force to Brumby, and there . . . they there slew five kings and seven earls."

The Old English poem also refers to ". . . the Northern heroes under a shower of arrows, shot over shields; and Scotland's boast, a Scythian race, the mighty seed of Mars! With chosen troops, throughout the day, the West-Saxons fierce press'd on the loathed bands."

When the victorious kings traveled back to Wessex a number of men from local Brunanburg tribes accompanied them.

They helped King Edmund subdued the rebellious Vikings of East Anglia in 942. He recovered "Five Boroughs" of Mercia in 943 and marched north into Northumbria. By 944, he brought all the Danish tribes back into subjection.

The reign of King Edmund, ended suddenly with his murder by a banished law-breaker, who stabbed him to death while dining with his troops and attendants at the village of Pucklechurch in the County of Gloucester about the year 946 and was buried in Glastonbury Abbey, Somerset.

Today, the County of Gloucester in England, has many descendants of those ancestors who came from Brunanburg with King Edmund.

Their Migration Experiences

Summary

DNA analysis of both the male and female genes has been of great help to show how the migrations and assimilation of populations of different tribes took place.

For example, even though most people of Semitic heritage of the Jewish Cohen or Priestly line going back to the time of Moses' brother Aaron shows a male Y-DNA trace that excludes most Northwestern Europeans, the same cannot be said of the female mt-DNA analysis.

The male DNA is passed from father to son while the female DNA is passed from mother to daughter.

Following the deportation of the Northern Kingdom, a female captive from Samaria could have married a male from one of the nomad groups that invaded the Assyrian or Median territory. It is possible that the married couple would continue to live with the group of Semitic people in that territory and produce offspring but they would have no Semitic genes; nor would they have any male offspring with Semitic Y-DNA.

Assimilation could take place however.

An Israelite male might marry a female from one of the invading tribes and have children while remaining within the same group. His male offspring would have Semitic Y-DNA.

In both cases, the outsider might assimilate into same tribe and or social group of his or her spouse.

This process of assimilation makes it possible for the introduction of people with a given genetic grouping into a region where another genetic group is dominant.

The first group may be a minority but still a significant part of the larger population.

Myth and Reality

Some Cimmerian and Scythian history may be based on mythical narratives or may be an embellished version of actual historical events.

Many of Britain's Celts believed themselves to be descendants of the Milesians who invaded Ireland from the Iberian Peninsula. While this account is mostly mythical, it may be an embellished version of actual historical events.

Recent genetic studies by Brian Sykes, Oxford University, suggests that many myths regarding Britain's ancestors are based on historical facts since many of the people of northwestern Iberia and Europe are genetically closely related to the Celts.

Their Migration Experiences

About the Author

Jess Browning is former Director of Global Trade, Transportation, and Logistics Studies at the University of Washington in Seattle. He has an MPA Degree from the University of Southern California and a Ph.D. from the University of Washington in Seattle.

At the local level he served on the Freight Mobility Roundtable; at the national level he served on the Transportation Research Board's International Trade and Transportation Committee; and at the International level he served as a U.S. Delegate to APEC's Transportation Working Group.

In retirement, he helped form a Consortium of eight international universities to do joint research and education in the fields of business, advanced technologies, logistics, and marine affairs.

Jess, a former entrepreneur, was engaged in manufacturing and global trade. He holds eight patents in environmental and process control equipment.

He believes that economic development takes place at many scales: From what takes place on the plant floor to what takes place in various regions of the world. He finds no difficulty in moving from one to the other to promote economic development.

Jess is an author of 6 books and has given many talks, lectures, and keynote addresses at home and abroad. He is married and lives with his wife near Seattle. Their 4 daughters have given them 6 grandsons, 4 granddaughters, 2 great granddaughters and more great grandchildren are on the way.

Their Migration Experiences

Acknowledgements

The author has been a great fan of Louis L'Amour for years. He respects L'Amour's work since his novels show a great deal of research in Geography and History. This author is quick to point out these facts to those people who seem reticent about L'Amour's works.

In this book, there are four passages in which part of the narrative in the story was inspired by the works of Louis L'Amour. They are adapted from short passages in L'Amour's novels: "The Tall Stranger"; "Callaghen"; "The Quick and the Dead"; and "How the West was Won".

Another source of inspiration came from the book The Extraordinary Voyage of "Pythias the Greek: The Man who discovered Britain" by Barry Cunliffe.

Further inspiration came from Bernard Cornwell's first book in the Saxon Tales series titled "The Lost Kingdom".

The inspired passages in all cases includes new characters while the dialogue, geography and time span are changed from what was written about the Wild West of the 1800s to the Near East of Anatolia in the period from 800 BC to 300 BC. Also from Western Europe in about 100 BC to Great Britain in 450-950 AD.

A lot of the source work in the book comes from the book "Ancient European Ancestors: The DNA, Archaeological, Historical, and Linguistic Evidence" by J. H. Browning, 2012, available online.

Their Migration Experiences

Index

Their Migration Experiences

Phoenicia, 14, 116
Phoenician, 91, 95, 98
Phoenicians, 95, 116
Phraortes, 20, 40, 41, 70, 71
Phrygia, 29, 57, 74
Phrygian, 29, 42, 73, 74, 75, 79, 81, 82
Phrygians, 29, 43, 74, 76, 79, 80, 81, 82, 85
Pillars, 89, 91, 117
Pilsner, 73
Pius, 101
plain, 13, 128
plains, 2, 13, 18, 45, 77
plan, 48, 59, 76, 111
planned, 49, 50, 77
planning, 3, 47, 107
plans, 50
plant, 135
plateau, 10, 39, 105, 108
Pliny, 118, 123
plodded, 59
plunder, 4
plundered, 43, 125
plunging, 90
Plutarch, 118
poem, 128
Poem, 98, 128
poet, 87, 97, 117
Poetic, 98

poets, 123
polar, 116
Polatli, 29
polemic, 86
politically, 12
Pontic, 43, 93
Pontus, 17, 22
Pope, 101
population, 93, 97, 131
populations, 131
Portugal, 89, 91, 98
Poseidonius, 90, 118
power, 9, 10, 11, 35, 42, 85, 89, 95, 115, 117
powerful, 4, 11, 13, 22, 82, 90
powerless, 109
Prague, 94
prayer, 36
prehistoric, 95
pre-Islamic, 13
presence, 18, 71, 79, 91, 94
priestly, 12
Priestly, 131
priests, 36
primitive, 123
prince, 71
Prince, 20
princes, 97
princess, 71
prisoner, 73
private, 12
problem, 55
proceeded, 99, 118, 120
proceeding, 38
proceeds, 29

progress, 43
promised, 14
promontories, 119
promote, 135
prophesied, 38
prophet, 38
Prophet, 14
prosperous, 105
Provence, 104
province, 69, 124
Province, 10
provinces, 11, 35, 69, 102
provincial, 10
Prtotohyes, 40
Pseudo-Scymnus, 86
Ptolemy, 100, 101
Pucklechurch, 128
purple, 110
pursued, 115
pursuit, 40, 70, 71
push, 17, 43
pushed, 78, 100
Pyrene, 89, 91, 92
Pythagoras, 87
Pytheas, 116, 123

Q

Quiberon, 115
quiver, 1

R

Ra, 8, 104
Ragau, 86

Rages, 56, 73
raid, 76
raided, 102
raiding, 112
raids, 102
rain, 46, 126
rained, 63
rains, 2
rape, 111
reality, 31
realized, 52, 81
realizing, 100
realm, 71, 117
rebelled, 70
rebellion, 36
rebellious, 128
record, 35, 116
recorded, 19, 20, 21, 22, 36, 38
records, 36, 38, 87, 90, 102, 118
Records, 85
red, 9, 30, 88
Red, 115
red-gold, 30
redhead, 111
refresh, 64
Refreshed, 60
refuge, 43
regiment, 12, 41, 57
region, 4, 7, 8, 10, 12, 13, 17, 18, 19, 22, 28, 38, 39, 43, 44, 56, 71, 73, 74, 85, 88, 89, 91, 92, 93, 94, 103, 104, 111, 118, 119, 124, 127, 128, 131
regional, 42

Made in the USA
San Bernardino, CA
18 September 2015